Glass exploded into the master bedroom, shards littering the hardwood floor.

Chelsey instinctively cried out and covered her head, ducking. Another crack of gunfire boomed and a bullet slammed into the chest of drawers behind her.

"Chelsey!" Tack bellowed outside the hall.

"Don't come in here!" He'd be an easy target looming in front of the window. "I'm not hit." Another projectile hit the bedroom door: "I'm still fine. Coming out."

So much gunfire.

One bullet after another. She couldn't be sure the Outlaw was the perpetrator. It might be the mass shooter, whose MO was a gun.

He wasn't the only one skilled with a gun.

"What's going on in there?" She glanced up and caught the edge of Tack's profile, peeping inside.

"Just getting my gun."

Another bullet entered the window.

She was trained for this kind of thing. *Channel the fear. Keep a clear head.*

Hard to keep a clear head when someone was doing their best to blow it off...

Jessica R. Patch lives in the Mid-South, where she pens inspirational contemporary romance and romantic suspense novels. When she's not hunched over her laptop or going on adventurous trips with willing friends in the name of research, you can find her watching way too much Netflix with her family and collecting recipes for amazing dishes she'll probably never cook. To learn more about Jessica, please visit her at jessicarpatch.com.

Books by Jessica R. Patch

Love Inspired Suspense

Quantico Profilers

Texas Cold Case Threat

Cold Case Investigators

Cold Case Takedown
Cold Case Double Cross
Yuletide Cold Case Cover-Up

The Security Specialists

Deep Waters
Secret Service Setup
Dangerous Obsession

Cold Case Christmas
Killer Exposure
Recovered Secrets

Visit the Author Profile page at LoveInspired.com for more titles.

TEXAS COLD CASE THREAT

JESSICA R. PATCH

LOVE INSPIRED SUSPENSE

INSPIRATIONAL ROMANCE

LOVE INSPIRED® SUSPENSE
INSPIRATIONAL ROMANCE

Recycling programs for this product may not exist in your area.

ISBN-13: 978-1-335-55488-8

Texas Cold Case Threat

Copyright © 2022 by Jessica R. Patch

This edition published by arrangement with Harlequin Books S.A.

For questions and comments about the quality of this book, please contact us at CustomerService@Harlequin.com.

Love Inspired
22 Adelaide St. West, 41st Floor
Toronto, Ontario M5H 4E3, Canada
www.LoveInspired.com

Printed in U.S.A.

The wicked, through the pride of his countenance,
will not seek after God: God is not in all his thoughts.
—*Psalm* 10:4

To all of my nieces, Chelsey, Ciara, Olivia, Katie, Myla
and Crimson—may you grow into and stay strong women
who seek the Lord and find your worth in Him alone.

A special thanks to my agent, Rachel Kent;
my editor, Shana Asaro; my friends and authors
Susan L. Tuttle and Jill Kemerer; my friend and
FBI contact "Mr. Anonymous" (anything I got wrong or
stretched is all on me!); and to my family. I appreciate
you all so much and couldn't do this without you.
Thank you.

ONE

You got the wrong guy.

Agent Chelsey Banks's stomach knotted as she recalled the carefully typed words of the letter she'd received almost three weeks ago revealing intimate details that proved her profile had led authorities in the wrong direction concerning a Dallas mass shooting. Dreading the truth that she'd somehow made a mistake, but unwilling to hide the letter, she'd promptly taken it to her section chief in Quantico, then asked for a personal leave of absence. She hopped a plane from Virginia to Gran Valle, a gorgeous rural valley town flanked by the Davis Mountains and, farther southwest, the Glass Mountains. She'd visited before and had been impressed with the peaceful community and quiet scenery.

But she was feeling no peace at the moment, not even on her nightly horseback ride. She'd been staying on Redd Rock Ranch for a little over two weeks now, and the guilt nipping at her bones hadn't ceased; it was like a moth gnawing away at an old sweater. Section chief Bob Wright had tried to assuage her guilt but agreed a reprieve would do her good.

The profile was solid with the information you had

*available, Chelsey. Not every behavioral analyst hits
the mark one hundred percent of the time. Not even you.*

But she had until this flub. Granted, it had led to
Marty Stockton—a bad man who had indeed done bad
things. But it hadn't been Marty who had opened fire
on an all-women's gym in Dallas one Saturday morning
over six years ago. And there was no absolving him of
the crime now. A week before the letter arrived at her
residence in Virginia, Mr. Stockton had been stabbed to
death in the penitentiary cafeteria. Which hadn't made
the news, and that meant the real killer might have had
personal knowledge on Marty Stockton and his life inside the pen that led to him sending Chelsey the letter.

Overwhelmed, shocked and humiliated, Chelsey had
no choice but to leave—maybe forever. If for no other
reason than utter shame. She'd prided herself on her impeccable record that led to the capture of vicious killers.
She was meticulous. Careful. And correct. How many
times had she said to colleagues, local law enforcement
and the press, "I don't get it wrong. You can trust what
I'm telling you is accurate." Especially concerning the
Dallas mass shooting. After Marty's arrest, Chelsey had
stood in front of dozens of cameras and assured them
they'd caught the right man, that the Dallas PD in tan-
dem with her profile had brought justice to families of
the fourteen gunned-down women and made the streets
safer.

Her career might as well be over. Time to eat crow.

It didn't matter that she'd been six years younger at
the time or one of the youngest female agents to become
a behavioral analyst with the National Center for the
Analysis of Violent Crime—or what most people knew
to be the Behavioral Analysis Unit, or BAU.

What mattered most to Chelsey and what would matter most to the sharks with cameras was that she'd been wrong after insisting, almost gloating, she'd been right. What had she missed from the interviews she'd been privy to and the files she'd analyzed? Something had slipped through her fingertips or the profile would have morphed and sent the DPD in another direction. They might have found the real killer, who for some reason wanted to revel in Chelsey's blunder now—over six years later. Why would a killer who had gotten away with murder and would have continued to be scot-free out himself?

He wasn't an idiot. He was clearly calculating and intelligent. It made no sense. Had he simply been waiting for the right moment to humiliate her? When she was just now taking her career to another level? Would he have even known this information? Since the mass shooting, Chelsey had increasingly been in the public eye on various cases, always worried the media might poke too hard and discover the truth about her, but hoping they wouldn't. There wasn't much of a trail. Not enough to send her slinking into the background.

Could this real killer have discovered her secret and that's why he was now willing to come out of obscurity— to harass her? What kind of monster would do that?

She rubbed Cortessa's dark mane as the chestnut mare guided her down the craggy trail. "You're a good girl, aren't you? No judgment from you. Just steady companionship." She sighed as the horizon displayed hues of orange, pink and violet, signaling that the sun was snuggling in for the night. The thick, arid May air swirled with enough heat to hint at a typical sweltering summer. But Chelsey had always loved Texas heat. If ever there was proof of a Creator, it was here in the mountains and valleys of West Texas. She missed Texas often, but her home and job were in Virginia now, where she could use the skills she'd gained by crooked means for good. For justice.

No one knew about her father. Her past.

They only knew what she wanted them to know. She had been bred for deception. But then, having a con artist for a father would do that. The early years, he'd called them games. How to pickpocket, how to spot a good mark. How to fake cry and play pretend. Chelsey had adored her father. He was bold and fun. Full of enthusiasm and life. Mom had died not long after she was born. Dad had been her entire world, and there was nothing she wouldn't do for him. He had always championed and encouraged her, even when she'd told him at eighteen she was done aiding him and going into law enforcement.

He'd seen it as a get-out-of-jail-free card.

And basically, it had been.

The last thing she wanted to think about was Dad. Except he'd called and let her know he'd be back in their hometown of Abilene for a few days and wanted to see her if she could take a little time to fly in from Quantico. She hadn't revealed to him that she was only four hours south on a weekend ranch that belonged to a family friend of her best friend since childhood.

Tack Holliday. A man completely opposite of her sophisticated father, who'd rather enjoy an espresso in an upscale city than hike through mountains or sleep outside in a tent and sleeping bag. Chelsey found her first smile of the day thinking of Tack. They'd met when she'd come to live with her aunt in Abilene at the ripe old age of five. Dad had told her he'd traveled for business—

more like escaping consequences from one scam to another city to plan another. Tack's mom and Aunt Jeanine had been best friends and attended the same church. It was Tack who'd taught her how to saddle a horse, to ride and to barrel race. Chelsey had won several blue ribbons, and it was a way to focus her energy and pass time missing her father, who popped in at least once a month. They'd even gone to the police academy together.

Now, Tack was a Texas Ranger and a good one, too. He was the epitome of cowboy, from his six-foot four-inch frame to his dusty boots and confident swagger. She'd often told him he looked like Blake Shelton minus the ability to sing a single note on key, and he bore a few more streaks of gray at the temples than the country artist. But working these kinds of jobs did that.

Cortessa clip-clopped down the, rocky trail where ranchers had trotted for generations. While the land was still worked, the owners had built a much bigger home north of this acreage but kept their first ranch house as a weekend getaway and place their eldest son, Dusty, lived when home from the rodeo. He and Tack had been good friends through the rodeo circuit and horse racing, and Dusty's family had become like family to Tack. They had been more than happy to offer the ranch, especially since Dusty was away on the bull riding circuit.

Tack didn't know she might need a place longer than a few weeks, since this wasn't vacation. But she couldn't bring herself to confide in her oldest friend that she was a fake and had come by her professional skills through nefarious means and was probably going to become a washed-up hack. Nor did he know the colossal secret she'd been keeping from him for almost twenty years. If he ever got wind of it…her friendship with Tack would be over in a split second, and she'd come to depend on their relationship over the years. She hadn't been able to bring herself to confess.

The small ranch came into view, the metal windmill spinning in languid circles in the evening breeze. The housekeeper was here. Izzy's beat-up Dodge Caravan was in the driveway. A white Ford truck had parked behind her. Probably her brother, Juan, the head mechanic on the ranch.

She slowly dismounted and roped Cortessa to the post, removed her bridle and bit, then rubbed her muzzle. "Be a good girl and I'll get you to the stable soon." The horse slurped from a water trough by the fence post.

She'd kept the side door to the home unlocked and entered through the kitchen, the scents of chili powder and cilantro hanging in the air from her late lunch. Izzy had brought her tamales yesterday. The house was quiet. Groceries sat on the kitchen island in plastic bags. Rivulets of condensation dripped from the gallon of milk. Izzy wasn't one to be idle or slow about her work. A sense of warning corded in her gut.

The kitchen opened into a rustic living space, and a hall to the left would lead to three bedrooms and two bathrooms. Quietly, she removed her boots and remained in sock feet. She didn't want the sound of clicking on hardwood to tip off a possible intruder, but something wasn't right.

A dull thump in the back of the house snagged her attention. Her gun was on her nightstand in the master bedroom. She glanced at the knife block and slid out the butcher knife, then inched down the hallway, her back against the wall until she paused by the first guest room.

The door was open. She listened, looked down and noticed boot prints, likely size twelve.

A gurgling noise drew her attention to the adjacent guest room.

"Shut up," a deep, husky voice growled.

Chelsey's hairs stood on end. Whoever had driven the white Ford had Izzy. She needed her gun! If she stayed quiet, she could slip in, grab it and hopefully aid Izzy in time. Heart pounding, she moved silently but stealthily until she hit an old, creaky joist. Her body froze, breath caught.

Had the man heard it? Blood rushed into her ears, causing her to hear nothing but sounds like a whirring fan. *Whoosh. Whoosh. Whoosh.*

It felt like a standoff. She feared moving, and he might be paused listening. One more step. She took it. Then another until she was almost to the master bedroom, the guest bathroom sandwiched between the two rooms. She began backing into the bedroom when a hulking dark figure charged her like a raging bull from the stall. He wore dark jeans and a long-sleeved black work shirt and matching cowboy hat. His face was covered in a navy blue bandanna like some kind of outlaw, and he clutched something in his hand.

A taser!

Chelsey bolted for her nightstand, but he caught her as she reached out for the butt of her gun and yanked her toward him. As she stumbled backward, she swiped his arm with the butcher knife. He growled and cursed. Chelsey wasn't going down without a war. In the next room, a life hung in the balance. She had to fight and live to save Izzy as well as herself.

The man released the back of her tank top, instinc-

tively grabbing his wounded upper arm, and she turned
and kneed him in the groin, sending him into a bent position. She swung the blade again, but he enclosed her
wrist with an iron grip and banged it against the closet
door until her only weapon clattered to the floor.

He hauled her up and thrust her onto the bed. She
bounced from the force but used the spring to focus
and kick him in the chest with both her feet. He toppled
backward into the closet door. Finally, she retrieved her
gun as a massive volt of electricity seared her ribs, stun-
ning her with a shocking jolt.

A fist connected with her left cheek, and then she
saw nothing.

Tack Holliday turned on the gravel road that led to the
Redd Rock Ranch. Up ahead the rugged fencing flanked
the big iron gate, holding two prominent *R*s turned in-
ward inside a metal circle. He'd been here dozens of
times to hang for the weekend with his buddy Dusty,
so when Chelsey had called inquiring about a peaceful
place where she could chill for a few weeks, he'd immediately thought of here, especially since she'd have
the place to herself. He'd called the Reddingtons to get
permission, which they'd gladly given.

Tack wouldn't mind owning a little ranch like this.
It had always been on his dream list. Nothing as massive as Redd Rock—the Reddingtons were one of the
leading beef cattle ranchers in the state of Texas. Tack
would be content with about a hundred acres and a little
homestead. A bachelor's life. Not that Tack didn't date,
but never seriously or with women who had intentions
of a permanent relationship. Tack wasn't the type to
string a woman along. He'd been raised better than that.

Plumes of dust billowed behind his Silverado as he pulled through the gate, noticing a van in the drive. Too banged-up to be a rental if Chelsey had changed her mind about getting one. Tack had picked her up at the airport, and she'd insisted she wouldn't need a vehicle right away since she wanted to enjoy the ranch and the amenities, like the pool, horses and hiking trails.

Who on earth had she made friends with in two weeks? Chelsey was friendly enough, but wary and often guarded. The woman had a hilarious side, but it only popped out with those she was most comfortable around. Like Tack. But even so, she kept things close to the vest even from him at times—like the reason for her request for time off and the need for a little out-of-the-way place to relax.

Chelsey was nothing if not a workaholic, laser-focused on her career as an FBI behavioral analyst in the BAU. She lived for the hunt, the traveling to consult for local law agencies. For putting tiny pieces together until they formed a complete picture that aided law enforcement in catching killers. The woman had a knack for it, he'd give her that. Savvy. Observant. Her mind never shut off or slowed down, and she hadn't taken a vacation in years. Not for more than a long weekend.

Three, maybe four weeks off? Didn't sit right. He parked behind the van as sirens blared and he caught the flashes of blue lights in his rearview. His heart rate kicked up and he leaped from his truck, gun and Texas Ranger shield in hand. He bolted for the front door as Chelsey burst out, the left side of her face red, her lower lip split and her eye beginning to blacken.

"Chelsey, what is going on?" he boomed. "Who did

this to you?" He sprinted for her as paramedics leaped from the ambulance and headed toward them.

"This way!" she shouted to the paramedics, ignoring Tack, as they rushed around him and inside. The sheriff's deputies approached and nodded when Tack raised his Texas Ranger shield then followed them inside.

"What is going on?" he asked again when he reached the hallway where Chelsey stood, a scowl on her face and her arms folded over her chest. Her long, dark hair was half out of a ponytail, and one of her huge brown eyes was swelling fast. "You need ice on that." He touched her cheek, and a paramedic pushed between them.

"Ma'am, are you hurt?"

"Clearly I'm hurt," she snapped, "but I don't have time to be upset about it." She huffed and waved him off. "Sorry. I'm fine. Really. I'm refusing medical treatment."

The sheriff's deputy scratched his head and pulled out his notebook as the medical team carried out a young woman with long, dark hair. She wasn't dead, but she wasn't conscious, either.

"Can you tell me what happened, Agent Banks?" the deputy asked.

Tack would like to know, too. His heart rate still hadn't settled.

"I came in from a ride. Around seven. Izzy Garcia— the housekeeper, lives in one of the bunks on the ranch— that's her gold van. Behind was a white Ford. Older. Didn't get the plates. I thought it might be her brother Juan, the ranch mechanic. But when I got inside, I could tell something was off. I moved down the hallway, and the intruder attacked me. We tangled. I sliced his left upper biceps with the butcher knife and went for my gun. By the time I reached it, he got to me with a taser."

"How bad's the burn?" the paramedic asked.

Chelsey sighed and raised the side of her white tank top, revealing a small red sear on her naturally bronzed skin. "Probably needs some ointment or whatever. I'm more concerned with Izzy."

"We won't know more until the doc sees her. But she's alive. Thanks to you, I believe."

"Did you recognize the intruder?" Tack asked. "Seen him before on the ranch?"

She described what he'd been wearing. "He looked like some kind of Wild West outlaw." She shuddered. "When I came to after he decked me, he was gone. I was afraid he'd gone back and finished the job with Izzy or abducted her. Maybe he thought he had killed her. She was lying on the floor, a long piece of a braided horse's rein around her neck. I loosened it, called in the cavalry. Thought I might need to start CPR, but she had a pulse. Faint."

Tack wanted to wrap her in a bear hug, but she'd frown on that. She was a tough woman and composed in public. Even now when pain glimmered in her eyes and the aftereffects of fear still tremored in her hands, she was taking charge, working.

"You say she lives in one of the old cabins on the ranch?" Tack asked.

"Yes. She's been living there and working as a housekeeper for the Reddingtons. Main house and the weekend ranch here. She's a sweet girl. Friendly. Early twenties. She's here on a temporary work visa from Mexico."

Tack's stomach constricted. He was working his own cold case right now. He'd joined the Unsolved Homicides division with the Rangers about four years ago. Company E. Moved from Houston, where he'd been working as a detective for the PD, to El Paso. "You said he wore a bandanna on his face? You get the color of his eyes? Anything?"

"No light in the bedroom. So no. Nothing he wore appeared expensive or unique. I saw the color of the bandanna because there was a light on in the guest room. I assume Izzy had turned it on, or maybe the killer wanted to see her clearly before he murdered her." She drew her eyebrows together. "Why? Tack, is there an outlaw strangler running around West Texas I don't know about?"

He turned to the deputy. "I'm going to take it from here." This county was in his jurisdiction. "I think this attack might link to unsolved homicide cases I'm working now."

"Cases plural?" Chelsey asked warily.

"Yeah." After talking more extensively with the deputies, they left them with one civilian crime scene investigator to process the scene.

Tack walked into the kitchen and opened the freezer, found a bag of mixed vegetables, and handed it to Chelsey. "For the eye. Keep the swelling down."

Chelsey accepted it and placed it on her cheek, wincing. "He's got a nice right hook, I'll give him that," she said, but her voice cracked. He pretended not to notice. Let her keep her false bravado and dignity.

"Show me the horse rein he left behind." He followed Chelsey to the guest bedroom closest to the bathroom. Lying on the floor was a braided brown leather horse's rein. He squatted, and the CSI handed him a pair of latex gloves. The catalog number card lay beside the evidence, and powder from printing remained. "You done with this?" he asked.

"Yes, sir."

Tack picked up the rein and studied it as Rosa Velas-quez's face came to mind. Dark hair but not black. Big brown eyes. Average build. Slim. Pouty lips. He glanced up at Chelsey, noticing she had the same features as the most recent victim in his cold case.

"Why are you looking at me like that?" she asked.

"You have puffy lips."

"Yeah," she smarted off, "I took one for the team here."

He smirked. "No, I mean in general. You have lips women pay for."

"Ugh, don't talk like that. It freaks me out. What is going on? And quit looking at my lips." She placed the frozen vegetables bag over them, amusing him.

He'd kissed those lips once when they were teenag-ers, but nothing came of it. Looking back, he was re-lieved. Tack had felt the deepest grief when he'd lost his youngest sister when he was only twenty-two and then his Houston PD partner—he'd been gunned down right before Tack's eyes only a few years later, and he'd been utterly powerless to stop it. Charles had left behind a widow and a two-year-old son.

Tack didn't see the point in investing so deeply in someone knowing that they were a vapor in the wind. Here today and gone tomorrow, leaving behind nothing but endless mourning and grief. Wasn't worth it.

Better to keep Chelsey as a close friend. Besides, she loved her job, the travel. The limelight. She wasn't one to settle down.

"I said stop staring at me," she insisted, but he heard the amusement. "Tell me about your cold cases."

Tack stood. "About four months ago, hikers illegally took their dog on the trails at Big Bend National Park, and while they were resting, the dog went to diggin' and uncovered a human bone. Did what any retriever would and brought it to them. They wigged out, of course— nothing like your lab bringing you a human arm. They called the ranger and the authorities. Long story short, they found the remains of four unidentified women. But one of the bodies had been buried recently. We had enough to photograph and show around. Rosa Velasquez. Twenty-three. Here on a temporary work visa from Mexico. Working as a nanny for a ranch about twenty-five minutes west of here."

"Did you get identification on the other three remains?"

Tack shook his head. "No dental records. No DNA matches. We know they were females about the same age and height as Rosa. What we do know by finding Rosa, only two days after her murder, was that she had ligature marks around her neck consistent with being strangled by a braided leather horse's rein. Like this."

Chelsey whistled low.

"Forensics found navy blue cotton fibers. You said he was wearing a navy blue bandanna over his face. Like an outlaw."

Chelsey nodded. "He was. Dark jeans and shirt. Black gloves. Cowboy hat. It almost fell off when I kicked him into the closet door."

"You kicked him into a door? Guess those kickboxing lessons paid off."

"You better believe it." She grinned and groaned. "My lip."

Tack's chest constricted at her injuries and at the fact that she fit the physical victim profile. Except she was pushing forty. But she could easily pass for late twenties. Only lines around her eyes creased when she grinned. But how would the Outlaw, as she'd described him, know she was here? She had no car. Went nowhere to his knowledge. Could he work on the Reddington ranch? If it was an employee, that narrowed down the suspect pool.

"Chels, does Izzy usually come by on Saturday nights and bring groceries? Is it her routine?"

"No. She said she'd be by on Mondays, except for this week due to extra cleaning for another client who was throwing a party later in the week."

Tack frowned. "Could he have thought he was coming after you and caught Izzy instead? You both fit his victim description."

"How? No one knows I'm here."

"Employees who work here know about you."

She stalked to the kitchen and started putting groceries away. Leave it to Chelsey to clean or chomp ice when she needed to think through something. He noticed a few envelopes on the counter at the same time Chelsey did. Izzy must have checked the mail. Chelsey seemed surprised to see the stack. Her face blanched as she touched a letter.

"What is it?"

Her head snapped his direction, and fear radiated in her eyes. "Nothing. It's nothing." She scooted the mail out of the way.

Tack knew better. Chelsey was hiding something. But why would she be getting mail at a ranch she'd only been staying at for a short time?

TWO

Chelsey's mind was rapidly firing scenarios, and it was too difficult to process them. A serial killer had gotten into the ranch and possibly mistaken Izzy for Chelsey. No. Tack's theory was wrong. It might not even be the same man he was after, even if there were similarities.

Because someone did know she was here.

The letter she'd tried to hide on the counter. Postmarked seven hours north of her in Dallas. Chills scraped down her back. The real mass shooter had already sent her one letter. Who else could it be from? There was no return address. Same blocky handwriting on the envelope as the last one.

How did he know she was here? Could he have mistaken Izzy for Chelsey? Doubtful, as he wouldn't know Tack's cold-case killer's signature. The mass shooter's temper was explosive, not calculated like the Outlaw, who methodically hunted, strangled and buried.

They could not be one and the same.

But she'd botched the profile. So what if he did have all the same traits as she assumed the Outlaw had or vice versa? Frustration and self-doubt muddied her thoughts, creating burning tears at the backs of her eyes. She laid the now-thawed vegetable bag on the counter much like her self-confidence—mushy and useless for the job.

If Chelsey had been the target and innocent, sweet Izzy had suffered in her place… The thought was unbearable. She'd already caused enough grief to families, including Tack's, though he didn't know her own father was at the helm.

The CSI tech let himself out after informing them they'd hear if something popped.

Tack gave her the eye that could make a stone squirm. His clear blues bored into hers, and an eyebrow raised in skepticism as his jaw tweaked, but he refrained from questioning her. He knew her well.

"Why are you here on a Saturday night anyway?" she asked, now wondering why he'd driven two hours from El Paso without even calling first. Not that she minded his surprise visit. She'd always welcomed company from Tack.

"I figured you were probably going stir-crazy, so I thought we'd stream the latest Denzel Washington thriller. And I picked up a box of tacos from Santa Maria's— 'course they're soggy and cold now. I'm glad I got the wild hair and headed down."

Chelsey was, too. Knowing Tack was nearby comforted her and infused a dose of security into her system. "I'm not really hungry anyway, and I think we have our own thriller going down, so how about I take some ibuprofen and you tell me more about your cold cases? You get a forensic anthropologist on facial reconstruction or carbon-14 dating?"

She replaced her thawing vegetables with a fresh bag of lima beans and then worked around the kitchen with one arm, grabbing a glass from the cabinet. Tack took the ibuprofen bottle from her hand, his nearness bringing a sense of steadiness. The smell of peppermint and his cool aftershave filled her nostrils. And also the hint of masculinity—a scent that couldn't be described or pinpointed but invoked a flutter in her belly. Not that the sensation was new by any means. Any woman would respond to his hard lines, alpha-male ruggedness and the kind eyes of a Southern gentleman mixed with the mischief of a cowboy. Tackitt Holliday was the epitome of Texas heat, from his gait to his boots to his deep molasses drawl that evoked charm—and flirtation when he wanted it to.

And he was her friend. Only her friend.

He placed two pain relievers in her palm and closed her fingers over them, covering her fist with his big, strong hands—the warmth soothing her clammy skin. "Hey, you know it's okay to be vulnerable with me, right? I know you're Superwoman and I love that about you, but I also know you're the same girl I carried two miles after you broke your arm trying to prove you were every bit as brave as Dell Farthing when you jumped across that stupid creek. Brave, yes. Dumb? Pretty much." He squeezed her hand with the heart of a man who cared deeply but pretended he didn't. "You cried the entire time on my shoulder, and I promised you then I wouldn't tell a soul. And if you're feeling like cryin' right now, honey, I won't tell a soul or judge a single tear."

No, he wouldn't. But she was far from Superwoman. She was a fake and phony and maybe God was punishing her for it, but she'd worked tirelessly to use the skills she'd learned from corruption for good. With every case she brought to justice, she scratched off a con she'd participated in with her father or one she was aware he'd done without her.

But the tally wasn't even close, and with each checkmark, she'd felt less absolved and even more guilty.

Then there was the horrific secret she'd kept all these years, solidifying her phoniness. Her hypocrisy. How could she share that or her latest glitch with the profile with Tack and take away the one thing he loved about her? "I'm not gonna cry. And I'm not a *girl* anymore."

His wicked grin revealed deep-set dimples in cheeks that were beginning to shadow with scruff. "No, ma'am, you are not. But the *man* in this ole boy says it's wiser to see you that way." He winked.

Even after all these years, Tack could bring out a blush in her like no other man could. And he was right in that he was far from a boy. He was most certainly all man. She slowly shook her head. "Anybody ever tell you you're a flirt?"

"Maybe a time or two. A little flirtin' never hurt no one." He released her hand. "Take your meds like a good girl." He winked again, and she swallowed down the pills.

"I beg to differ. Roy James killed Tanya Moore up in Clinton, Illinois, because she flirted then didn't make good on those harmless little words."

"I retract my statement, Agent. A little flirtin' among normal human beings never hurt anyone." He opened cabinets until he found the coffee. "How about some caffeine while I lay out the facts, and then you can give me a loose profile."

Could she? What if she got it wrong?

"You think the Outlaw mistook you or targeted Izzy?" he asked as the coffeepot began gurgling and the smell of rich brew filled the kitchen. "And let's hope the media doesn't get wind of our little nickname. I hate giving killers some kind of infamous name."

"Agreed."

Victimology was a safer route to discuss. She'd bypass a profile and concentrate on the deceased, then hope it was enough to help her make an educated guess on who the unidentified subject might be, but she'd really rather not even try. Except Tack would know something was up, and she wasn't ready to reveal she'd failed at what she loved most—her job.

"You said the one victim you could identify, Rosa Velasquez, was here on a work visa and had been employed on a ranch as a nanny. She fits the same physical type as Izzy and myself. Izzy's also here on a work visa. The unidentified victims might have also been here on temporary visas. Did you run a search to see if any women with work visas had turned up missing?"

"Believe it or not, dear, it ain't my first rodeo, and that's exactly what I did."

She didn't doubt Tack, but her type-A personality couldn't help itself from following up. "Anything turn up?"

"One woman went missing, but she was in her late forties and didn't fit the physical type he's targeting. So my next thought was he could have targeted women here illegally and there would be no way to trace them. No photos. No DNA in a database or fingerprints. Not even dental records."

Chelsey began putting away the groceries that weren't ruined. So much for the vanilla ice cream. She chucked the container full of now liquid in the trash. "Sadly, they would make easy targets for a predator. If he had stalked or harassed them prior to the murder, they would feel helpless—unable to go to authorities because they had no legal citizenship. Most people who hire illegal immigrants do so because they can pay them less, pay them cash and not include insurance. They'd feel like a nuisance approaching an employer for help and ultimately powerless, which is exactly how the Outlaw would want them to feel."

Which made him a man who craved control, dominance and power. But he picked weak victims. That was no real challenge or equal match compared to a strong woman. And that told her, beneath the power trip, he was weak himself. She couldn't say why yet…but she wouldn't throw any ideas out. She didn't want Tack running with them to be wrong later. It would ruin his record, his professional reputation. And she refused to be the reason why.

"Like killers preying on prostitutes. Generally, their families have written them off or don't care."

Chelsey nodded and poured a cup of coffee. "The world's outcasts. Everyone needs someone to trust, to rely on, to keep them safe." She'd always trusted herself, but now…she wasn't sure she could. "If our speculation is correct and these were the kinds of prey he was hunting, these women had no voice. No hope. No help."

Tack scowled. "We help them now, then. We don't let this Outlaw outrun the law."

"Just don't go half-cocked. I could be wrong about this guy and his targets."

"Since when do you cop to claims of being wrong? Since when have you ever been wrong about this kind of thing?"

Since her educated guess cost an innocent man his

life. "Nobody's perfect," she snapped. "Sorry. I'm beat-up and cranky." She let a little laugh escape and Tack grinned, but she saw disbelief in his eyes.

"You remind me of Poppy when you talk like that."

Chelsey adored Tack's sister. She worked cold cases for the Mississippi Bureau of Investigation and had recently solved their youngest sister's murder. Poppy also worked with the wife of her friend Cash Ryland. Chelsey had met him years ago at a conference, and they'd kept in touch. Small world. She'd helped him work a profile that caught the killer who'd been targeting him and his now wife, Mae. Least she'd gotten that one right.

"I'll take that as a compliment."

"Not sure I meant it as one," he deadpanned. "Redirecting the subject here. The lab's still working on trace evidence, but with this new attack, I think it now makes sense to get a forensic anthropologist."

She sipped her coffee. "How have we not been called in? You had a mass grave."

"We Texas Rangers can work a case, too," he said good-naturedly but with a hint of firmness, letting her know he wasn't handing this over to anyone. "The BAU might have the corner on the analysis market, but that doesn't mean other agencies don't have skilled profilers."

Heat filled her cheeks. She hadn't meant to belittle his or the Rangers' skills. "Sorry. Again."

Tack clipped her chin playfully. "Two apologies in a day. You goin' soft on me, Banks?"

She rolled her eyes and averted her gaze. She had one apology she'd owed him for years.

"Hey, your skills are welcomed. Needed. I've been hitting dead ends until now. Rosa has no other family here."

"Who reported her missing?"

"Employers at the River Valley Bend Ranch where she'd nannied reported to immigration that she hadn't shown up to work one day—I checked the records to verify."

Chelsey grimaced. Why call immigration after one day? That was odd. Either they were the kind of people who expected no less than punctuality and professionalism or someone knew she wouldn't be back.

"You want to go up there Monday morning and talk to them yourself."

Leave it to Tack to read her thoughts. She did normally prefer to be present for interviews, to observe body language and ask questions to provoke particular reactions that would help her. Dad had taught her a wealth of skills concerning tells. The Bureau had, too.

She was torn. The part of her that thrived on doing her job ached to perform, but the failed part of her whispered she could mess up again, that she wasn't as good as she thought—as others believed—and wanted her sidelined. "You feel good about their answers?" she asked.

"I did at the time."

"Then why do you need me? You've got a good gut."

"You saying I'm fat?"

"I'm saying I trust you." And she wasn't sure right now that she trusted herself. Not to mention she had an unopened letter she was itching to get to and dreading at the same time. "But you can do me a favor. Cortessa is on the post outside. Could you stable her for me?"

He paused but then nodded. "Sure." When he walked out the back door, she waited until he was at the tack shed and involved, then she donned a pair of latex gloves and opened the letter with shaking hands.

Surprised to find this? I thought you would be. It's not hard to track a person. Maybe I should have gone into the FBI. You only have to be half-good at the job. I noticed there's no media attention yet. Guess you and the agency are sweeping it under the rug. Maybe I need to drop an anonymous tip.

You're not worth your salt and not much of a ramrod, are you?

She found a plastic gallon bag in a drawer by the oven and slipped the letter inside. She'd have to give this to her section chief, who would put at least two of her colleagues on looking into the case. How humiliating for them to clean up her mess. Probably be Duke Jericho and Vera Gilmore. They were top tier in Chelsey's opinion, and they were friends outside work. In some respects, Duke reminded her of Tack.

Her neck and shoulder muscles tensed and spasmed. How had he found her? And why taunt her? That continued to needle her. There was a motive. An endgame.

She sent a quick text to Vera letting her know another letter had come and that she would be sending it to the lab and calling their section chief, Bob, later to inform him.

A few seconds later, Vera replied with a caution to be careful and that they had her back.

But what might they be saying behind it? All the things in this letter? Because the shooter was right. She wasn't worth her salt or much of a person in charge. She'd gotten work done but the wrong work.

She sighed and pressed the heel of her hand to her good eye. Her head pounded, and her jaw ached. The pain reliever needed to kick in ASAP. Tack wanted her help on this case.

Could she give him sound advice without second-guessing herself?

She groaned and tucked the letter in the drawer under the plastic wraps and aluminum foil. Tack would be back any moment.

She finished putting away the groceries and wiped down the counters, then went to the back bedroom and flipped on the light. She hadn't gotten a good look at what had transpired in here. After studying it, she switched off the light and went into the master bedroom and inhaled. She closed her eyes and inhaled again, picking up a lingering scent. Faint but there. Unable to place it, she huffed. It was familiar. And foreign.

"Chels?" Tack called.

"In the master bedroom."

His boots clicked along the hardwood, and he entered the room. "Whatcha doin'?"

"Smelling. Close your eyes. What do you smell?"

He obeyed and inhaled deeply. "Cooking spices. That soap you use—hint of vanilla—leather and...hossy-stink."

Chelsey snorted, but he'd nailed it. Musky, like someone who'd been around animals a lot. "Like a ranch hand?"

Tack opened his eyes and nodded. "Like a ranch hand. By the way, the hospital called. Izzy's awake."

"What are we waiting on, then?"

"Hossy-stink and your kind of smell-good," he joked and led her out of the house. "Why haven't you rented a car yet?"

Because she was here hiding.

But someone had found her. Maybe more than one killer.

Tack and Chelsey rode the elevator to the second floor of the Gran Valle Regional Medical Center and strode to the nurses' station as he retrieved his identification case, which held his other Texas Ranger badge, silver plated over bronze. He kept the silver badge made from a Mexican cinco-peso coin with his suit coat. He showed it to the charge nurse, and Chelsey refrained from showing any creds. Odd. She lived for revealing her work. It was more than an identification process to get what she needed. It was her identity in general.

Something was off, and he wondered if it had to do with that piece of mail that had withered her before she tried to hide it from him by sending him to the stable. He might not be as perceptive as Chelsey, but he was no greenhorn.

"Tack?" A Hispanic man in dirty jeans and a Western shirt approached, his worn boots as filthy as the cowboy hat he removed. Juan Garcia. They knew each other a little from the times Tack had visited with Dusty on weekends. But he hadn't made the connection between Juan and Izzy until just now. He'd never met Izzy. Oh, man. Poor guy.

"Hey, man. It's good to see ya—unfortunate circumstances." Tack shook Juan's hand and glanced at Chelsey.

Juan followed his trail of sight, and his eyes widened. She was bruised enough to notice. "Are you the one staying on the Redd Rock Ranch? The woman who saved Izzy's life?" Before she could answer, he enveloped her and kissed her good cheek. "Thank you so much. I don't know what would have happened if you hadn't shown up and rescued her."

Tack noticed Juan had not only been working on machinery but he'd been around cattle today. The musky smell smacked his senses.

"You're welcome. I'm glad I arrived at the ranch when I did. Things might have turned out differently." Chelsey broke away from the embrace. "You work for Redd Rock?"

"*Sí*. Yes. I work for Mr. Reddington. Fix machinery. For nine years now." Pride shone in pitch-black eyes.

"Do you live on the ranch or elsewhere?"

"In the main cabin on the east side of the property. They built new ones with the new house."

"Did Izzy mention anyone bothering her, following her or even giving her the creeps?" Chelsey asked.

She wasn't supposed to be at the house tonight. She was either followed or someone knew where she would be. But did they know Chelsey would be there? Why park his truck behind Izzy's van if he knew someone was around who might be able to get a plate number or identify it?

"She never mentioned anything to me." He raked his hand through his hair. "She did tell me she saw him."

"She talked to you?" Tack asked. "Maybe you should have led with that." What on earth were they waiting on?

"I called the sheriff, and he said he'd get in touch with you. You were taking over."

"She say what he looked like?"

"She was confused and scared. They gave her something to settle her down."

"How do you two know each other?" Chelsey asked

as they hurried toward Izzy's room, the smell of bleach and someone's dinner wafting in the chilly, sterile hall.

"Sometimes I come down on weekends when Dusty's not riding bulls and acting like he's sixteen and not almost forty." Tack laughed. "And I've taken some downtime on weekends here myself. Gotten to know some of the guys."

Enjoy the ranch life vicariously. Maybe he'd have one in a few more years, if the price was right, or when he retired. Tack loved catching bad guys, loved bringing closure to families, which was what drew his interest to the Unsolved Homicides unit. After Cora vanished, it had devastated the family and caused distance. Especially between Poppy and their parents. He had kept thinking if they would only find her or know what happened, then they might be able to unpause their lives and push Play again. Families needed closure and forward movement. Though the grief remained either way.

Tack still grieved Cora. Still grieved his old partner, Charles. It was too deep. Too agonizing. Work kept it buried. Weekends helping ranchers with backbreaking labor kept his mind off it, too. It was at home in the quiet of his house that he had to face the loss. The never-will-be-agains.

"We need to get a sketch artist out here," Chelsey said. "Rangers have one. Can you call him or her in?"

"Her. I'll do it now." Just as he plucked his cell phone from his pocket, alarms sounded and "Code blue" came across the speakers. Nurses scurried like ants after their bed had been stepped on.

"That's Izzy's room," Juan said.

They bolted but were forced to remain in the hall.

Chelsey's attention was drawn toward the stairwell, and Tack followed her line of sight. A doctor was exiting.

"Tack, how many doctors do you know who wear grimy cowboy boots to work?"

"None," he said, retrieving his weapon as his pulse spiked and he began pushing through medical staff to the stairwell. Inside, the doctor's boots clicked louder, picking up pace. He must have heard Tack's footsteps. "Stop!" Tack ordered. "Texas Ranger." But the footfalls increased, banging on concrete. He was jumping stairs. Moving faster.

Tack heard the steps behind him. Smaller but fast. Chelsey.

As he hit the first floor, the stairwell door was closing. He barreled through, searching for where the fake doctor ran to, but it was a bust. Tack entered the men's room to his left, slowly peeking to see feet underneath the stall doors.

Empty.

He began kicking them open one at a time. The Outlaw could easily be standing on a commode. Each metal door banged against the stall, echoing throughout the bathroom. Finally, he reached the last one, gripped his gun and kicked.

Empty.

He huffed and exited the men's room. Chelsey jogged up beside him. "Local police are here. I've had security called and asked for video footage. Come on. Let's get upstairs."

They rushed into the elevator and bounded out on the second floor, taking a hard left and hurrying to Izzy's room. Juan slumped on the floor outside her room, his hat in one hand and his hanging head resting in his other hand. Local police were inside the room.

"Juan," Tack said softly.

"She's gone. They asked me to step out."

As in gone to surgery, or… "Gone?"

"She's dead, Tack. They found her smothered with her own pillow."

Chelsey looked at Tack and grimaced. "The Outlaw. He's taken another life."

Tack nodded. The only witness who could ID him or at least give them a description was now dead, and Tack was back to square one.

Except… Chelsey. His lungs turned to iron, and his stomach balled into concrete fists. She might not have seen his entire face, but once she had time to think and clear her head, it was possible she'd remember minute details. She'd always been uncannily aware of her surroundings and people. Even when it appeared she was paying no attention, she could tell you the shoe color of a stranger who had walked by five minutes ago.

Somewhere in that brain, she'd have more details and a profile that would get him closer to catching the Outlaw. Or they'd get a major break and see his face on hospital footage.

But she wasn't only a witness for Tack. She was a loose end for the killer.

"I'm so sorry for your loss, Juan," Chelsey said. "Is there anyone we can call for you? Get you something?"

He stood and secured his hat on his head. "No. My family is back home in Puebla."

"I know you want to grieve and I hate to stall that," Chelsey said, "but are you sure you haven't seen anyone hanging around Izzy? Noticed any other ranch hands or employees eyeing her? Did she go anywhere at all? Have a girlfriend she ran around with?"

Juan pawed his face. "She was friends with all the women working at Redd Rock. Don't have any idea what they talked about. They're women—no offense."

"None taken. Thank you. We'll follow up if we need to. Again, I'm so sorry."

He nodded and trudged toward the elevators. Once he was gone, Chelsey and Tack entered the room; Tack talked with the detective and let it be known he had jurisdiction. Crime scene techs arrived and began working the hospital room and poor Izzy. After Tack instructed the techs to follow up with him, they studied the room for themselves.

"Gran Valle Regional would be the obvious option to take Izzy. The Outlaw didn't get far enough away before he heard sirens and realized she wasn't dead. He knew he had to get the job done before she woke and talked. He knows she saw him, could give a sketch artist his profile, or he wouldn't have made such a desperate move, Tack."

"Any person with half a brain knows there are video cameras all over, except inside the rooms. Somewhere between Juan leaving and the code blue, he found a doctor's coat and slipped inside. He was quick and efficient. Does this help you with building a profile? What's your take?"

Chelsey swallowed and darted her gaze across the room, and her cheek twitched. "I—I can't say for sure."

Tack frowned. What was going on? "I didn't ask you to say for sure. I asked your opinion based on what's transpired. What kind of killer could we be looking for?" He refrained from asking if her sudden vacation, letter in the mail and now this obvious display of keeping her thoughts close to the vest had anything to do with something that had happened at Quantico recently, but if she hadn't confided in him yet, she wouldn't if he blatantly asked. He stayed quiet, agitated and frustrated instead. "Give me something." Could be about the killer. Could be what was going down with her.

Chelsey must have understood his subtext. She relaxed her shoulders and stared at Izzy's lifeless body. "He lingered long enough to see medical personnel rush in to attempt to save her. He knew he only had a brief window of time to get away clean, but he stuck around. Coming at all was a high risk. Cameras. The possibility of getting caught stealing a doctor's coat. Being seen by a nurse entering the room. Being seen by Juan." She sighed and rubbed her temples. "It thrilled him. To see them helpless to save her but to take all the risks and win. Which he did."

"God complex? Does he think he's invincible? Can't get caught? Smarter than law enforcement?"

Chelsey inhaled deeply through her nose and ran her finger along the bedrail. "Likely. He's arrogant and prideful. He takes his time with his victims, even with the strangling. A pillow? Why not steal a syringe and inject air into the line? He stole a coat for camouflage. He enjoys the torment—but… I can't be sure. I could have it all wrong." She refused to meet his eyes and pointed to the door. "Let's watch the footage instead."

He followed her into the hall and caught the doctor he'd seen earlier. "Excuse me, could you tell me if you or someone else worked on Izzy Garcia?" He showed his Texas Ranger badge, and the doctor nodded.

"I'm Dr. Pelican."

"HIPAA doesn't apply anymore. Can you tell us if she said anything to you or if you heard what she might have said to her brother Juan?" Tack asked. "He said she talked to him."

Dr. Pelican cocked his head. "The poor woman's hyoid bone had been broken in her initial attack."

"Hyoid bone?"

"It's a U-shaped bone and serves as an attachment structure for the tongue and for muscles in the bottom of the oral cavity."

"So what does that mean?"

Dr. Pelican's eyebrows tweaked. "It means, Izzy Garcia never spoke a word to anyone. She couldn't have."

THREE

"Why would Juan Garcia lie about Izzy claiming to have seen the killer?" Chelsey asked as a myriad of ideas fired in her brain.

"That's a good question," Tack said, rubbing his scruffy chin. "One we'll ask, but first let's review the footage and see if we can get our own identification on this guy." Security had led them to the offices to review the video.

"Hey, that reminds me," Chelsey said as she sat in a metal chair in front of a monitor station with several black-and-white screens revealing movements, "about the forensic anthropologist. I have a friend at Baylor who could drive down, work out of one of the university labs here. Charlotte Westcott. She's pretty, too—if you're in the market." She and Tack didn't talk much about their romantic lives, mostly due to the fact neither of them had much of one. Tack less than Chelsey. Their careers had become their significant others.

"Is that your way of asking if I'm involved?" he teased and shifted on the uncomfortable chair as a security officer brought them small foam cups of steaming coffee. Probably wouldn't taste great, but it would do its job.

"No." Was it? Did she want to introduce Charlotte to Tack as a love interest? "It's my way of lighting a fire under your behind to get a forensic expert on those bodies. It could be months longer before you know anything concrete. Every lab in every state is backed up. People just can't quit committing crimes already." She huffed, and he smirked.

"Well, it would put us out of a job."

She might already be out of a job. Not by firing but the fact she wasn't sure she could slink back into the BAU with her head high. Not the woman who was a crack profiler. The woman who didn't make mistakes. Didn't miss things. But right now, women were dying and would continue to die at the hands of a serial killer. She couldn't allow that. So she'd work with Tack and build a profile, but her nerves were frayed and her insides rolled in on themselves at the thought of being wrong again.

"As much I love what I do, I'd be okay with that." She sipped her coffee and wrinkled her nose. "I can't think."

"Need some ice?"

"Absolutely." Something about the cold crunching of ice chips helped her think straight. Drove her colleagues nuts, but Tack had never seemed to mind. Whether it was studying together for a biology test or thoughts about the world and faith, Chelsey liked her ice. Preferably in small, square chips. Thankfully, most hotels carried the very kind she worked with best. And hospitals. "I'm going to find a machine."

"I'll go. You start reviewing." He stood. "This chair doesn't do anything good for my back. And don't say a word about me getting older. I ain't quite forty yet. Let me have a couple more years before you start in."

"I was going to start with the pops of added silver to your temples. I'll save the backaches for next year." She tossed him a smug expression and refrained from adding how much those little flecks added to his appeal. He had a healthy ego—no point puffing it up further.

"I'm a firm believer in going au naturel." He waved her off with his hand and his ridiculous remark and left the security station.

Chelsey signaled a young security officer who was sitting a few desks over—Marcus. "Can you give me the hall and stairwell leading to the second floor? Rooms two hundred to two twenty? I'll need to see it starting at an hour and forty-five minutes ago. I also need footage of all entrances starting thirty minutes ago." When the killer had escaped their grasp. "That includes employee entrances and restricted areas that are on cameras."

"Yes, ma'am." He went to work, and she rolled around the scenarios. Why had Juan said his sister told him she saw her killer when she couldn't speak? If she'd written it down, there would have been evidence in the hospital room or Juan would have handed it to them when informing them that his sister had identified or described her killer. Why lie? Wouldn't he have known they'd enter the room and realize she had no voice?

A sudden thought hit. Had all the victims' hyoid bones been crushed? That might be the Outlaw's reason for his MO. They were all victims who had no voice. By taking away their ability to speak, he ultimately robbed them of their voice. That played into his thirst for power and control—but didn't fit the invincibility angle or his need to be thrilled by risky scenarios.

Where was that ice?

"Okay, Agent Banks. I have everything cued up for

your viewing. If you need anything else, I'll be at my desk." Marcus nodded graciously and left her to it. She began with the footage of the stairwells leading to the end of the hall where Izzy's room had been. How did he know which room was Izzy's?

"You're smart and clever, aren't you?" she murmured. "You would have seen or heard the sirens then followed at a distance, lingering in the halls without being noticed. Which means you blend in easily when you want to. You watched and waited then made your move. Opportunity and calculation combined." Just like a con man. Just like Dad.

"How did you know this about me?" Tack growled in a menacing voice. Chelsey startled and frowned.

"Warn a person before you sneak up on them and scare them half to heaven." She laid a hand over her heart and huffed. When she was deep in her profiling process, she tuned out everything and everyone.

He ignored her retort and handed her a cup of ice loaded to the brim.

"I'll forgive you since you brought me brain food."

"Technically, I brought you solid hydration. Do you think the Outlaw knew Izzy personally? How is he connected to her?" He sat beside her and shifted in the chair, a divot forming on his brow, then he stood, hovering over her to see the monitor. He really hated that chair.

"Possibly. She went out of her norm—to the grocery store on a day she normally didn't. Could have caught his eye in the parking lot and he followed her. That makes it more difficult to narrow down a suspect pool. However, if he killed your other victims, then he had to have knowledge of their visa status or the fact they were here illegally. That's calculation, not opportunity presenting itself."

At this point, Chelsey was ruling out the mass shooter as her attacker and Izzy's killer. But he was still out there and a possible physical threat, though it appeared he'd rather play psychological games with her. And it was sadly working.

"Right there." She pointed to the recording of the west side entrance. "That man is wearing the same boots I saw, but he's got his head turned and he's wearing a cowboy hat." She looked up. "Marcus, can you trace this man's steps throughout the feed for us?"

Marcus nodded and strode over to use the computer, clacking keys and moving footage forward until the man entered the elevator. They switched to that feed, but the man's head stayed down. "No facial details, but he's tall and built like my attacker. He keeps his hands in his pockets." She slipped another chip of ice into her mouth and crunched. "Why? Is there something telling that he wants to keep hidden, like a tattoo or scar?"

"Maybe he's giving off an air of being nonchalant," Tack offered.

Chelsey cocked her head, studied his posture. Wide shoulders, no slouching. "Typically people put their hands in their pockets due to a lack of confidence—insecurity. But look." She pointed to the screen. "His thumbs are out. That tells me he's highly confident." Which fit her initial guesses about him. "You see this type of stance often with people of high rank or status." She glanced up at Tack, who was standing in the exact same position—hands in pockets, thumbs out. She grinned.

"What?" he asked, unaware of his stance. She nodded with her chin toward his waist and he noticed, removing his hands from his pockets. "It's comfortable."

"It's confident cowboy swagger," she replied and refocused on the man on the feed. He wore a long-sleeved shirt. In this heat, that meant he was accustomed to it, likely worked in it. "He's hidden almost every feature, as if he expected authorities to search the feeds. He wanted no telling signs. He may have one or multiple tattoos on his forearms or hands. Also, he may have wanted to keep any hairs covered—DNA. Which means he may be in the CODIS and knows we could get a match on him." Once again, clever and calculated.

"If we find any DNA in Izzy's hospital room or off the pillow, we'll be sure to run it. But you know it can take some time. The Combined DNA Index System isn't like on TV, where it pops up in five seconds."

Wouldn't it be nice if it did.

Tack leaned in farther, his chin right above her head as she examined their unsub further. "He has a cowboy gait."

"So does about every man in West Texas. And cowboy hats are the norm." Once a man broke in a good hat, he rarely parted with it. Chelsey doubted they'd find the Outlaw's. He might have taken it off to slip into the room as a doctor, but he wouldn't leave it behind. They continued to watch as he stepped off the elevator onto the third floor. He disappeared behind a swinging door. "Where does that lead?"

"Supply rooms," Marcus said.

Where he snagged the coat. "Get security to comb that area for any trace evidence." As they continued to watch, he emerged in the white coat and ducked into the stairwell. The next set of cameras caught him waltzing right past Juan Garcia, who was scrolling through his phone, oblivious, then into Izzy's room. "He hesitates. Back it up. Watch."

Marcus rewound the footage.

"He's striding with purpose, head down, but he spies Juan in his periphery and pauses. Maybe he knows Juan can identify him and is rethinking it…or maybe he wants us to know he knew he was there and yet had the audacity anyway." Chelsey crunched into ice chips. "He's brazen. He parked right behind Izzy's old van knowing there was a possibility of someone—maybe even me— seeing it." Which she had. She could kick herself for not getting the tag number.

"Are you saying I'm looking for an arrogant killer who loves the thrill of almost getting caught but believes he won't because he's uncatchable?"

Her past mistakes told her not to make a solid conclusion so soon, but this guy had proven more than once what kind of man he was, what kind of killer. Still she hesitated to give him a profile that would aid in his search. "Perhaps," she said as a knot pinched in her gut.

"Perhaps? Chelsey, give me something I can work with."

Chelsey drank the melting ice water, letting it cool her burning throat. What if she was wrong? "I'm not ready to spin what little thread we have into a tapestry yet." She could not have another profile backfiring. Another stain on her previously impeccable record. Lives depended on it. Tack's career depended on it. The last thing Chelsey wanted was Tack's name being smeared because of his connection with Chelsey and her profession.

Or her personal stains that could smear him.

"Agents—" a security officer stepped inside "—we

have a media frenzy outside. They want more information on this Outlaw. They know a woman died at his hands. In our care."

Chelsey's name for him.

The only other person besides Tack who knew she'd called him that was Juan. He must have talked to the press after he left the hospital. So much for not letting their personal nickname for him get out. Now they were here wanting answers. She didn't have a single one.

"We're going to have to go out there, Chels," Tack said. "Me and you. Working a case together. Who would have thought."

And now if anything at all were amiss, Tack would go down with an already sinking ship, in the form of his oldest and dearest friend.

What had she gotten him into? And could she get him out?

"Ranger Holliday, can you tell us if this present case regarding Izzy Garcia connects to any unsolved homicides you might be working? And has your company invited Agent Banks here in a professional capacity?" A blonde reporter thrust her microphone forward, clearly hoping for a sound bite.

The press and the media attention came with the territory. He'd learned quickly how to be diplomatic and not lose his cool.

Except the one time he did.

There were online videos of that horrible moment in his life, when he'd been caught at his worst on camera after Charles had been gunned down. He glanced at Chelsey. While Tack wasn't one to enjoy the spotlight, Chelsey had always thrived in it. He could count dozens of times he'd watched her on national news. Always poised and sharp. An appropriate response to every question and a cool head.

But now she was standing silently, as if camera shy.

"Agent Banks, are the wounds on your face from the Outlaw killer? Our sources say you called him that. Ranger Holliday, can you confirm a serial killer called the Outlaw is hunting women in West Texas?"

"How long?"

"Who might be in danger?"

"Do you have a profile, Agent Banks? Did you see the killer?"

"Who might be doing this?"

"Ranger Holliday, is this murder in connection to the remains found a few months ago in Big Bend National Park?"

Reporters fired questions like a six-shooter. Tack stepped up to the plate since Chelsey hadn't even swung. "We don't have any concrete answers or connections yet. Agent Banks is not here in regard to my case, but she has offered her expertise on the murder of Izzy Garcia and is consulting with the Texas Rangers. I trust her solid and stellar performance, and we will work diligently and swiftly to bring this killer to justice."

Chelsey's face blanched, and she swallowed hard.

"Do you have anything to add, Agent Banks?" the blonde asked again.

"Not at this time. Thank you." She pivoted and entered the hospital building, leaving Tack surprised and unsettled. Whatever was going on with Chelsey had struck her deeper than he'd initially thought.

"I have no further comments at this time. Thank you." He left the press unsatisfied and demanding more information and stalked after Chelsey. He found her perched on a bench in the atrium, her thumbnail jammed between her teeth.

Cautiously he sat beside her, stretching his long legs out in front of him. "I'm not a behavioral analyst, but I can observe and put together facts."

She remained silent, staring ahead into space.

"I know you're not here on vacation, because you never take vacations. You don't do peace and quiet for more than a long weekend. You get stir-crazy. You thrive in the chaos of criminal activity, putting order to it and ticking off the box that's labeled *justice is served.* You're hiding. Not sure why, but I know it involves something that was or will be in the public eye and you dread it, or you'd have rushed to the limelight out there."

"You make me sound like an egomaniacal camera hog." She scrunched her nose at his observation.

"No. But you like control, too. You oversee the scenario, the profile and the media. You didn't control their narrative, didn't set the record straight out there, and that's not like you. I imagine it's eating you alive right now."

"You have no idea what's eating me."

Because she hadn't confided, which stung. He'd been her friend the longest, and he'd never once judged or betrayed or proven he was untrustworthy.

She looked up then, into his eyes, and for the first time the depth of her fear hit him in the chest. "You shouldn't put that kind of stock in me, Tackitt," she whispered. "Shouldn't have told them anything concerning me."

He ran his tongue over his teeth, thinking. She must have swung and missed. For a normal person, it would be a setback. But Chelsey wasn't a normal person. She was her own worst enemy. Her own worst competitive rival. She took things hard, especially concerning herself. When she hadn't mastered the barrels after a week, she'd kicked one down and thrown a nasty hissy right there in the arena. Mad at herself for not being perfect. In a week.

Who knew what had happened in her career. She had too much pride to tell him. But she needed to know that she could. Should already know.

"I believe in you, Chelsey. And we're gonna get this guy. So suck up what's got you unsure and off your game. 'Cause I need that brilliant mind and Holmes-like observation skills." He held her chin to force continued eye contact. "I need you on this with me. No matter what you might have done that feels like a strikeout. You're my hard hitter. Batting a thousand. You understand?"

She nodded. "Batter up," she mumbled.

"That's my girl." Reminding himself she was not a gorgeous woman who could make him feel things on a highly emotional level. Emotions he refused to let his heart engage. Because they led to heartache. Just being her friend, the closeness they shared in camaraderie was dangerous. But something more? That would be his death warrant. And he didn't have time to die a slow death when he had killers to catch and incarcerate.

"Why don't we head back to the ranch and get some shut-eye? Tomorrow you can call this Charlotte friend and we'll pay Juan another visit. We now have two questions for him—why lie and why go to the press?"

Chelsey stood and rubbed her lower back. "I could use some sleep. I was sore from the long ride yesterday and today before I went all smackdown with this Outlaw character."

She strolled beside him to his truck. A disturbed feeling raised hairs on his neck, and he paused, scanning the parking lot.

"What is it, Tack?"

"I'm not sure." Sure felt like someone lurking in the shadows, invading their space and waiting for another opportune time to strike again. "Chelsey, I don't want to scare you." Not that much did. The woman ran headlong into danger. Had profiled and caught notorious killers. "But you're now the only one who could be of any help finding him, and by now he probably knows you're not only law enforcement but a profiler at that."

"Makes him no different than any other criminal."

"I beg to differ. Most killers try to outrun you. This guy...he's probably going to find you a most formidable foe. The ultimate risk and thrill. He ain't gonna try to outrun you, honey. He's gonna run right for ya."

She shuddered and opened the truck door. "I'll watch my back. Like I always do. I can take care of myself."

Tack slid into the driver's side and started the truck. "I know. But you're distracted and not yourself, so perk up. That's all I'm saying. And know you now have another set of eyes watching. Mine."

She nodded and leaned her head against the seat, resting it and her eyes.

"I need you to do what you do better than anyone else."

A soft sigh escaped her lips. "Okay. I need to see the crime scene at Big Bend where the bodies were uncovered and to talk to everyone you already have. Rosa

Velasquez's employers and friends. Get me the case files. And I need to go by the grocery store."

"You gonna cook me something tasty?"

"I'm gonna need more coffee than what Izzy purchased. If you're real nice to me, I might make you shells."

"I love those things." Nothing but taco meat, cream cheese and spices stuffed into large jumbo pasta shells with taco sauce and cheese. His mouth watered just thinking of them. "But how nice we talking? Like let you run lead on this case or kiss you good-night kind of nice?"

She laughed and opened her eyes. "Pretty sure these lips are unkissable with the big fat split."

He'd beg to differ.

"And it's your case. I don't want it. I'm here to consult. Low-key. Fade into the background."

As they pulled down the long, dusty road that led to the ranch, lights blared up ahead. News vans and reporters were staked out like vultures. "So much for the background, friend." He sighed and stepped from the truck with his Ranger badge. "Private property, folks. I'm tired, so maybe give me some grace from having to arrest every one of you fools."

One of the cameramen lowered his video camera. "Is the Outlaw a serial killer? And how long has he been killing? We deserve the right to know. The public needs to be aware."

Where was his reporter? Cameramen didn't ask the questions. They filmed it. Tack didn't have the time to deal with this mess. "I can't say anything right now. But as usual, be careful, pay attention to your surroundings and lock doors to your homes and vehicles. All precautions anyone should be adhering to anyway. Now, off the property."

He and Chelsey ignored jabs, gripes and further probing, but eventually the media trickled off the private property, although he had no doubt they were congregated on the road near the driveway waiting for them to leave, to follow, to scavenge information.

Inside, Chelsey flipped on the lamp and drew the shades for privacy. "You hungry for real? I can put out some sandwich stuff, or I have a few leftover tamales Izzy made me yesterday."

"Tamales sound good, but I have to admit I'm at the age I can't eat spicy this late. So I think I'll make a turkey sandwich and call it good." His smirk also came with a warning to refrain from old people jokes. Seemed like yesterday he was jumping cliffs into the river and riding bulls. He'd slip a disc if he did that mess now. How Dusty was keeping up was beyond him. Though last time they'd talked, he was considering retiring. But neither of them wanted to quite give up the fight on age.

Chelsey headed for the kitchen, but Tack stopped her. "Rest. I can whip up sandwiches. I know how you like it. Mustard, no mayo. No pickle, extra cheese."

She laughed, but it was tired. "I won't argue. You wanna take the guest room tonight? The one that wasn't a crime scene. No point going back this late." She frowned. "I cut him. Pretty good. I imagine enough for stitches. I'd say let's check hospitals, cover all bases, but if he's a ranch hand as we suspect he might be, then he'd probably have access to someone who could do it. He was right-handed, and that's the arm I sliced. If he's in the system, we'll get DNA. In the meantime, I don't see him stitching himself up with his left arm."

Tack slapped turkey on white bread and added romaine lettuce. "We could always greet people with slaps to the right arm instead of handshakes. See who winces."

Chelsey laughed through her nose and sat at the island as he loaded her sandwich with three pieces of Colby-Jack cheese and a dollop of spicy mustard. He slid the plate over and licked a dot of mustard from the side of his hand. She bit into her sandwich, and they ate in silence a few moments.

"How's your family?" she finally asked and sipped from a bottle of water.

"Better than they've been in a long time. Poppy got engaged this past Valentine's Day. She's truly happy, and I'm happy for her. Wedding is set for December. I might need a plus-one. It's so easy to get around the conversations about settling down if I have you as a buffer."

Chelsey picked the crust off her bread. "Why aren't you settled down?"

"Work?"

She stuck out her tongue and made a sputtering noise.

He cocked his head. "Yeah? What's your reason?"

She tucked her tongue back inside her mouth. "Work," she mumbled. "But tons of people work like us and have families."

"Work like us?" He doubted that. Chelsey worked from can to can't because she loved it. Tack loved his job, too, but sometimes it was a way to ignore loneliness.

"Well, maybe not to the same degree. Fifty hours, then. I just… I don't want to be married. I like my freedom. I like full control of the remote, and I don't need anyone eating the last of something. I want the last ice cream sandwich, bowl of cereal or Coke."

Tack laughed. "You basically said you don't want to get married because you're selfish and refuse to share."

She threw a piece of crust at him, hitting him square in the nose. "Shut up."

"I'm calling baloney on that." Chelsey wasn't selfish. She gave tirelessly to the Bureau, she helped anyone in need and she had always dropped anything and everything to be there for Tack, like when Cora disappeared before they knew she'd been murdered. They'd just graduated college together and were about to enter the police academy, but he'd postponed it and she had, too.

He'd begged her to go on, but she wouldn't go without him. They'd spent those few months together until spring, and then they'd entered the police academy together. It was after that they'd parted ways. He'd stayed in Houston, and she'd gone to Dallas and then later the FBI academy.

"Call it baloney. Call it anything you want. I'm going to bed." She slipped off the stool and tossed the paper plate in the trash.

He watched her leave the kitchen and called out, "Hey, Chels, you want this *last* chip? Okay, then." He shoved it in his mouth, crunching extra loud, and laughed when she responded with another demand to shut up.

After cleaning up the kitchen, he headed for the front door to get his emergency bag. He'd learned long ago to keep extra clothes and a toothbrush in his truck. Some cases lasted all night. He turned the knob just as the blast of gunfire, shattering of glass and Chelsey's guttural cry reached his ears, and his heart shot into his throat.

FOUR

Glass exploded into the master bedroom, shards littering the hardwood floor. Chelsey instinctively cried out and covered her head, ducking. Another crack of gunfire boomed, and a bullet slammed into the chest of drawers behind her.

"Chelsey!" Tack bellowed outside the hall.

"Don't come in here!" He'd be an easy target looming in front of the window. "I'm not hit." She was calculating a plan, but one glance at the shards of glass and at her bare feet told her it would be a bloody one. She spotted her riding boots near the bathroom door. She snatched a hanger lying on the end of the bed and used it to draw the boots within reach and grabbed them.

In a crouching position with her heart hammering against her chest, she shoved her feet into them. Another projectile hit the bedroom door. "I'm still fine. Coming out."

So much gunfire.

Like the type used in the mass shooting. One bullet after another. She couldn't be sure the Outlaw was the perpetrator. It might be the mass shooter, whose MO was a gun.

Staying low, she inched around the bed to retrieve her own weapon she'd laid on the nightstand before washing up for bed. He wasn't the only one skilled with a gun.

"What's going on in there?" Tack called from outside her room. She glanced up and caught the edge of his profile, peeping inside.

"Just getting my gun."

Another bullet entered the window, hitting broken shards of windowpane still attached to the frame. Chelsey tucked herself in front of the nightstand, forcing herself to breathe and not panic. She was trained for this kind of thing. *Channel the fear. Keep a clear head.*

Hard to keep a clear head when someone was doing their best to blow it off.

"Can you get to me?" Tack asked.

"Never in my life have I wanted to get to you more," she said, hoping her terror didn't override her attempt to be cool under pressure.

"You flirtin' with me, honey?" he asked, but his deep concern and a hint of anxiety were woven in every word.

"You wish," she said through a groan as she pushed off the nightstand and darted toward the door, staying in a crouched position, her leg muscles burning. As she reached the door frame, a bullet splintered the lintel and Tack yanked her out the door and into him. She smacked against his chest with a thud and another groan.

She scrambled onto the floor next to him, her chest heaving. "You call in backup?"

"Not my first rodeo. If we stay put, unless he decides to come in guns blazing, we're okay until the sheriff arrives. The sirens'll scare him off."

She could only hope. If it was the Outlaw, and he'd figured out she was a federal agent, he might not go anywhere, might even stick around longer and enjoy the risk. However, if it was the mass shooter—he definitely knew who she was, but he'd be more apt to run. He had an endgame she wasn't sure of, and getting caught right now wasn't it.

"You get hit with glass?"

"A few small cuts on my arm. I'll be fine."

He grimaced. "FYI, until I have a better handle on the situation, consider me your houseguest."

"Stay as long as you like." Not having to be alone gave Chelsey's iron lungs some breathing room, but that meant Tack was putting himself in danger, and it wasn't fair for him to risk his life when he didn't know the truth about why she was at the ranch in the first place. Two possible killers coming after her doubled his chances of injury, and he deserved to be aware. Didn't mean she wasn't feeling anxiety over telling him about her mistake and how it had led to the death of a man doing time for a crime he didn't commit.

No time for humiliation to rear its head now. Sirens squawked and Tack began inching his way down the hall. Chelsey followed suit.

A deputy hollered, "It's clear, Ranger Holliday."

"Stay here. I'll get the door."

Just for good measure, Chelsey covered him from the hallway as he rushed like wind to the front door. For being a big guy, he had graceful movements. Deputies entered, and Chelsey met them in the small foyer, explaining what happened.

The forensic guy, Mike, was back and he tossed her a flat look. "Should I just set up shop in the backyard?" he asked.

"Maybe," she offered with a sarcastic bite, and he went to work.

"I have flashlights in my truck. Let's poke around." Tack motioned for her to follow him outside. Deputies were combing the area for any evidence. There were a few large trees around the home, but after that it was all pastureland and hill country that stretched for acres.

She shivered, but not from the weather. It was balmy, and stars lit up the night sky for miles. But no sign of the shooter.

"They'll get shell casings and the projectile. Maybe they'll be able to match it to a gun owner."

"Maybe," she muttered and wrapped her arms around her middle. "I have to tell you something, Tack." She braced herself. Might as well tell him in the dark, where she couldn't see his face. His judgment. His regret from telling the press he trusted her implicitly. Hard to trust someone who'd made a colossal oversight somewhere and messed up royally. She couldn't even trust herself.

"Okay," he said quietly, warily.

Chelsey inhaled and peered out at the pastureland. "Remember Marty Stockton—the mass shooter at Warrior Women Gym in Dallas?"

"Yes, you called gloating with that one. Slam dunk. What about him?"

"He died in prison a few weeks ago. Murdered by an inmate."

"That's not your fault, Chelsey."

"Yeah, it is." It was all her fault. "A few days after his murder, I received a letter at my residence. From the actual mass shooter." She told him about the letter, going to her section chief and taking time off to reevaluate everything.

He stood silently as deputies and crime techs worked the scene. "How do you know you didn't get the right guy? Maybe whoever wrote the letter saw an opportunity to toy with you."

She shook her head. "Because the real killer gave me detailed information about how he entered the building, where he opened fire first and how many women fell to their deaths. He described in detail the mask he wore, which we never made public. Marty Stockton said he was home that morning sleeping in. Turns out, it was true."

"How did he get your home address?"

"I don't know. My plan was to come here, figure things out and take another look at the interviews, photos and profile, but then plans changed and I've had little time to do anything." She turned and faced him. "If you're going to be on me like white on rice, then you need to know that whoever fired on us tonight might not be the Outlaw. You might be in twice as much danger and so…now you know."

Tack raked a hand through his wavy hair. "Why would you think the shooting tonight wasn't connected to the—" He froze, hand still on the back of his head. "The mail you didn't want me to see. What exactly was in that envelope?"

Chelsey's insides sputtered. "Another taunting letter from the mass shooter. He knows I'm here, and I have no idea how. I mean, it wouldn't be terribly difficult to figure out my personal residence, but no one knew where I was leaving for except my direct superior and a few colleagues, and Duke and Vera wouldn't tell anyone where I was going."

In the moonlight, Tack's jaw twitched, and he grimaced. "I want to see that letter now." He stalked to the house, and she trailed after him. Inside, she handed him the plastic bag with the letter inside.

"Well, at least your brain is half working." He already had gloves on in case they had found any evidence of the shooter outside. "You should have told me the truth all along." He continued to mutter about her lack of mental capacity, and she let him. She'd earned the verbal barbs. The news had shaken him. It had shaken her, too.

He read the contents. "What are you going to do?"

Continue to let the dark truth sink in—she'd made a grave error and might not be worth her salt anymore. Maybe never had been. She was nothing but a con artist herself. "It needs to go to the lab in Quantico and be tested for prints and trace evidence, though the first one came back clean."

His nostrils flared, and he huffed. He had every right to be irked. "Any other killers follow you to Texas that I need to know about?"

Okay, that was enough. She jutted out her chin. "No! Because up until now I've hit the mark and sent every murderer to prison, where they belong." And now innocent ones, too! She lost her steam and slumped. "Now, I don't know. Who knows how many innocent people might be in prison because of me. I know nothing, clearly. The author of that letter is right. I'm not nearly as good as I think." She blew a breath of frustration and collapsed into a chair at the kitchen table, cradling her aching head in her hands.

Tack's boot clicks closed in, and his hands gently gripped her shoulders. "I'm sorry. I don't mean to be cranky. I'm frustrated. One or maybe two killers want you dead. That alone ruffles my feathers. But you didn't trust me enough to tell me, for whatever reason. And that, Chelsey, that flat out makes me see red."

She slowly raised her head and peered up into his eyes. "This has nothing to do with me not trusting you, Tack. It's about you not being able trust me." Tears singed the backs of her eyes. "I can't even trust me," she whispered. "I can't help you catch the Outlaw when I'm not sure of my abilities anymore."

He slid a chair out and turned it around, straddling it and resting his arms on the back. "Everybody makes mistakes."

"Not me. Not when it comes to the job."

He let out a heavy sigh. "You're too hard on yourself and always have been, but we're not going to get anywhere arguing that point. So let me say this. I trust you. I trust your judgment. I know you better than anyone. Let's start over brand-new. Is there anything else you're not telling me that I should know?"

Yes. *Oh, Lord, help me.* "I've told you everything about this case that I know." She'd condemned herself. Tack had the right to know his family had been swindled and that her dad had stolen his two brothers and Poppy's college funds, likely to pay off Chelsey's college debt.

He framed her face with his warm hands. "No more secrets. Promise me?"

Her insides twisted into pretzels, and she struggled to look him in the eye. "I won't keep another thing about the mass shooter from you. I promise." But she couldn't promise anything else, and she hated herself to the very core because of it.

He hesitated and studied her, as if he didn't believe her but desperately wanted to. She'd put him in the same position her father had put her countless times. She knew her father was lying, and yet she wanted to believe every word from his deceitful mouth. Finally, Tack mussed her hair and gave one solid nod. "Okay."

"Okay," she mimicked, but nothing was okay. His family had been taken, and telling him wouldn't bring any solace, resolution or hope…there was no way to retrieve the money they'd lost, and she had no way to even prove what Dad had done on paper—no solid evidence. He was good at covering up a paper trail. Maybe not telling him and his family was a mercy. Nothing was black-and-white. Too much gray.

Tack stood. "Do you still have access to the digital files of the mass shooting? I'd like to see them."

"Not all of them, but I can get everything."

"We're gonna need a boatload of coffee." He laid his hands on the table and leaned down, nose to nose with Chelsey. "If anyone can work two cases and come out on top, it's you. And it's me…yeah, I'm bragging. I'm pretty good."

She laughed at his attempt to lighten the mood with his false arrogance. "I'll make coffee." And she'd fill a cup with ice. Then she needed to make a phone call to Duke Jericho, a colleague at the Behavioral Analysis Unit in Quantico.

She got the coffee brewing and called him. He answered on the second ring.

"And what brings a call this time of night, Banks?" Duke's gravelly voice had a soothing effect on her but could be menacing to a person of interest.

"I got another letter." She told him about the newest development and the Outlaw's attacks, Tack's cold cases and the fact she needed help, which was hard to ask for when she was used to handling things herself.

"You need us to come out? Or just me? You got your hands full, Banks."

"Ain't that the truth. No, I just need you to email me the rest of the files."

Duke was silent for a few beats. "I will, but expect me and Vera to continue to look into this on our end. More heads together, better the outcome."

Was that a jab at the fact she liked to work solo when building a profile? "Okay." She had no choice but to accept the aid. "Keep me posted, and if it gets hairy, I may take you up on the extra backup."

"Consider it done. I'll have the files to you in a jiff."

After hanging up, she waited about ten minutes until she heard her phone ding. Files. She and Tack began poring over them and discussing the Outlaw. The next thing she knew, the sounds of ranch hands, horses and clinks of farriers working on horseshoes awoke her. She was still at the kitchen table with a crick in her neck, and her left arm she'd used as a pillow was numb.

Tack had fallen asleep on the couch and had jolted awake as the sun tiptoed onto the horizon, revealing a glorious Sunday morning in the shades of pink and orange. After cleaning up in the guest bathroom, he'd come out and heard Chelsey stirring in the master bedroom.

Nine more hours of shut-eye would have done them both good, but they didn't have time for further rest; they didn't even have time to attend church. So he took the extra few minutes this morning to reflect on the Lord and His goodness as Tack enjoyed His beauty in nature. He'd read a chapter in Matthew from his Bible app and breathed a prayer of thanksgiving and for wisdom in this case, and for Chelsey.

Something had been wonky from the get-go, but the fact she'd hidden real threats ached like his bad knee on a rainy day. He had no idea who had attempted to kill Chelsey last night. Two killers. One felt invincible, and one was unpredictable. What kind of killer revealed himself when he'd gotten away with murder? Tack was flying blind, and it had his teeth on edge. Thoughts of inadequacy and powerlessness swept through his veins, leaving him chilled, and brought back that horrible night when Tack had tried to negotiate with the man who'd taken his partner hostage in the convenience store— a robbery gone bad to worse.

Tack had employed every tactic he'd learned and had available for Charlie's release. But it was there in Darnell Robinson's eyes. He wasn't going to let Charlie live before he jumped in his old Impala and squealed out of the parking lot. They'd caught him before he made it to Mexico, but Charlie had lost his life and Tack had delivered the tragic news to his widow, who had a two-year-old son to raise alone. But Tack had been there as much as he could, walking through the grief with her, only to be reminded of the void in his own soul from his youngest sister's death. He'd been raised to be a strong man who could handle anything by a military father who had never cried, bended or broke.

Tack had done all those things when Cora went missing. But he'd done it alone, even hidden from Chelsey, which was why he couldn't stay mad at her for keeping the fact she'd messed up a profile from him. It made her feel weak and incompetent. He understood those feelings. Understood her reasonings. But he'd been alone, broken when Charlie died. No one to witness his weak tears.

He still hadn't cleaned up the debris those losses had left on his heart. Never would. Some things couldn't be fixed. Couldn't be made right or new.

"You look like you might be sick," Chelsey said, startling him. "You feeling okay, Tackitt?"

"Yeah," he said and pawed his face, shaking loose from what he wrestled with most. "How you feeling?"

"Like I fell asleep at a table. Like I was nearly killed twice yesterday and have more work than hours in the day. Other than that, I'm five by five."

Tack puffed at her military phrasing. One she'd heard his own father use often when asked how he was doing. Just fine. Best as possible. Tack wasn't quite the man his dad was. But he'd take that to the grave. "You hungry?"

"Not really. But I know I need to eat. You had anything yet?"

"Coffee with some cinnamon roll creamer that's entirely too sweet." He turned his nose up and studied Chelsey. Dressed in jeans and a flowy top. Hair pulled into a severe ponytail that hung down her back. She'd used makeup to hide most of the purple underneath her left eye, and she'd inked a soft pink lipstick over her split lip to cover the injury.

"I like it." She poured a cup of coffee and a generous helping of creamer to make her point. He rolled his eyes as she sat across from him. "I called Charlotte—my friend who's a forensic anthropologist. She's agreed to fly in later tonight and said she'd call and handle using the lab at the university to work. It would help my profile if we could identify those other three bodies. Find out if they worked on ranches and note the locations to triangulate a geographical pattern. No killer worth his salt is going to travel long hours with a body in his trunk.

Not that it hasn't been done, but if I had to guess, I'd say his hunting ground is less than a hundred-mile radius."

Tack pushed back his chair to make room for his legs. Crossing one leg over his knee, he said, "He's clearly familiar with Big Bend. He picked a private, off-the-beaten-path location to bury the bodies and it took some time and effort, so he was aware he'd have privacy and time."

"Good thing hikers ignored the rules and brought their dog. You may never have found the bodies."

Tack agreed.

"I'd like to see the burial site."

"Let's get some breakfast and I'll make a call to the chief of visitor and resource protection. Jerry Allen. He's good people."

Chelsey gripped her mug with both hands, the steam pluming. "First I want to talk to Juan Garcia."

"There's a little place downtown by the historical museum that makes the best southwestern omelets this side of heaven. Let's get a bite and get to work."

"I'll get my gun and purse." Chelsey dumped her coffee down the drain and scurried to the master bedroom while Tack holstered his weapon and grabbed his wallet and keys before they headed toward Gran Valle's downtown district.

After breakfast they headed to Redd Rock Ranch's main house, where the Reddington family resided in a large A-frame home with three floors surrounded by indigenous landscaping and a circular drive.

Tack rang the doorbell, and a few moments later a plump woman with a thick, dark braid opened the door. "May I help you?"

"I'm Tack Holliday. Friend of the Reddingtons and a

Texas Ranger." He showed his badge. "Can we come in and speak with them?"

She eyed the badge and Chelsey, who showed her FBI creds and introduced herself. The housekeeper led them to the massive kitchen, where the scents of bacon and coffee lingered from their own late breakfast.

Ruben Reddington and his wife, Laurel, sat at the table leisurely drinking coffee. Ruben glanced up from his laptop and grinned, skin like aged hide cracked and dotted with sunspots. He removed his reading glasses, but his Stetson remained on his head. Laurel's silver hair was pulled back in a barrette, and she wore long slacks and a short-sleeved pink sweater.

"I was wondering when we might see you in a professional capacity," Ruben said. "Awful what happened to you, ma'am, and to Izzy. And on our property."

Laurel clutched her chest. "It was awful. We sent a flower arrangement to the hospital, but we haven't heard anything new from Juan. Not since about eight last night. How is Izzy?"

Tack exchanged a glance with Chelsey. "Ma'am, Izzy died late last night." Tack gave them as much information as necessary.

Chelsey cleared her throat. "Does Juan work on Sundays?"

"Ranch doesn't know the difference between one day and the next," Ruben said. "We break for church, and our pastor holds a small outdoor service for ranch hands in the evening. But I haven't seen him this morning. I suspect he'd be in the barn working on broken-down equipment."

"Do you know if Izzy and Juan were close? I assume he had influence getting her this job," Chelsey said.

Ruben nodded and closed his laptop. "Juan is a good man and hard worker. When he told me his sister needed a job, we told him we'd make room."

"Izzy was precious and very devoted to her work." Laurel twisted her cross necklace.

"She have any friends? Talk about a boyfriend?"

"No," Laurel breathed. "We didn't talk much about personal things. She was shy. At least around us. She didn't want to do anything to jeopardize her job. I told her to relax. She was doing an excellent job. I don't know how to contact her parents or even if she has any." Laurel dotted her eyes with a linen napkin. "I feel so responsible. This is our land. Our home. Nothing like this happens in Gran Valle."

Until it did.

And it had.

FIVE

The large metal building on the ranch came into view as Tack's truck jostled them due to the bumpy, gravel road that led to the former mechanic's pit. Equipment, a row of ATVs and old machinery littered the yard.

"Is that his truck?" Chelsey asked.

"I don't know. Can't remember." Tack parked behind it and surveyed the surroundings. The sun had fully risen and had no intention of shying away from projecting its severe heat. About fifty feet west, ranch hands bustled around the stables. Tack inhaled the earth, hay and sunshine.

"Well, if he isn't around, we can talk to some of those guys. See if they knew Izzy. I'd like to inspect her cabin as well. I need a sense of who she was, and maybe we'll catch a break and find something that will help us conclude where she'd been recently." Chelsey exited the truck, keeping her hand on her holstered gun.

Tack followed her into the large shop. The concrete floor was unswept and littered with tools and broken-down ATVs and golf carts. "Juan?" Tack's voice bounced off the metal walls.

Nothing.

"Maybe he's back at his bunk," Chelsey offered and waltzed out of the garage, heading straight for the pens where cowboys were breaking horses. Farther out, ranch hands moved round haystacks and sprayed weeds.

Tack noticed their eyes lingering on Chelsey, and while she showed nothing but cool professionalism, the slight pulse in her cheek revealed she'd noticed and it wasn't welcome.

"Ma'am," the bigger and older man said as she approached and revealed her creds.

"I imagine you've heard about Izzy Garcia by now," she said, taking the lead and establishing authority in order to convey she wasn't an object to appreciate but here in a federal capacity. Being her oldest friend meant he could read her fairly well. He observed the men—either of them could be a killer. Everyone was a suspect to Tack.

"Yes, ma'am. We're real sorry, too. Izzy was a good woman." He removed his cowboy hat and held it to his chest in a display of respect. "How can we help?"

"Your names and jobs would be a nice start," she said and drew a small notepad and pen from her blazer pocket.

The older cowboy nodded. "Jay Cartright. I'm the point rider for one of Reddington's herds. This is Gerardo. I'm training him."

"Gerardo?"

"Sanchez, ma'am," the younger cowboy replied. Short and stocky. Didn't have the same build as the man on the hospital footage, but Jay Cartwright was six foot or six-one and muscular. Broad shoulders. Slim waist.

"Where were the two of you last night around six thirty to seven thirty?" Tack asked.

"Bunkhouse," Cartwright replied. "Ate dinner around seven. All of us."

Chelsey cocked her head and squinted. Was she not buying it? Tack hadn't seen a tell. "How well did you know Izzy? She lived in a cabin near the bunkhouses. She eat meals with you? Sit by fires at night?"

"Mostly she worked at the main house. Occasionally, she had dinner with Juan. Quiet."

"Boyfriends? Anyone take an interest in her beyond male appreciation?" Chelsey asked.

Cartwright shook his head. "Not that I seen." He glanced at Gerardo, and he shook his head, agreeing.

They thanked them and got back inside the truck. The gravel road would lead farther back to the bunkhouses and the ranch manager's cabin, where Izzy had been living. The Reddingtons hired out a ranch manager from a local company, so the cabin had been vacant before Izzy moved in. With her cabin being farther away from the bunkhouses, she'd had more privacy. Also meant she'd been more isolated.

Barbed-wire fencing, scrub brush and cacti flanked the dusty road as they forged through the ranch acreage to the bunkhouses. "I love Texas mountains," he murmured as he feasted on the scenery.

"Me, too. I miss Texas, to be honest. That's why I called and asked if you knew a place I could retreat awhile. It'll always be home in my heart."

"Once Texas takes over your heart, it never leaves. Why didn't you stay with your aunt in Abilene?"

"I needed to be alone. With my thoughts. With everything that happened. I'm sorry for not being straight with you, Tack. It's just…making that kind of mistake when you never make them hits hard."

Seemed like there might be more, but if she didn't want to talk about it, that was fine. She was at least talking some now. "Everyone makes mistakes."

"Again. I don't make those kinds. Anyway, back to Texas. When you gonna get your own ranch?"

"When I have more time to tend one. And when I have more money." He grinned. "Just a small one, you know?"

Chelsey nodded. "I wouldn't mind living in a place where I could have a few horses. I like being out away from everyone. I see people too much."

Tack agreed. "Yeah. Bad people. You live in a quiet town." Woodbridge seemed nice the few times he'd visited her.

"It is. But it's not Texas heat and Texas mountains. Cowboys and ranches." She snickered. "You know when I was about sixteen, maybe seventeen, I dreamed of marrying a cowboy."

"Riding off into the clichéd sunset?"

She hooted. "No. Just… I don't know…living quietly and escaping the world." She sighed as they neared the bunkhouses. "But the truth is you can't escape the world and all the darkness it hosts. That's a pipe dream."

"Gotta live in it. Wade through it. Hit it head-on."

"Best one can, I guess," she said.

Tack killed the engine and shifted in his seat. He'd never once heard her talk of living on a quiet ranch away from the world. What did she want to escape? What had she been keeping close to the vest all these years? "You certainly have plowed your way into it, swinging bats of light at it. I always wanted to be what would make my dad proudest."

"Nothing more impressive than having a son as a

Texas Ranger. Toughest of the tough. Strongest of the strong. Bravest of the—"

"I get it," he said through a laugh. But she was far off base. If she knew how weak he felt, and how powerless. So much less of a man than his father would ever believe. Tear shedder, wounded heart. He liked her view of him. Just wasn't accurate. "What did your dad want you to be? Or did you get the 'be anything you want to be' speech?"

Chelsey heaved a sigh. "Dad has always supported whatever I do, but I suspect he'd have loved for me to go into the family biz with him." Her warm eyes grew dark, and she grimaced as she shrugged a shoulder. "Guess the song is true. You don't always get what you want."

"I can't see you as a bigwig corporate consultant like your dad, although you do like to travel, and your dad has been everywhere."

"Yeah. Yeah, he's always running here and there." She slammed the door. Guess her family dynamics were as complicated as his. As probably every person's on the planet. He'd learned there was no normal or perfect family. His job had revealed that.

"Which one is Juan's?" she asked, nodding at the buildings in front of them.

The bunkhouses were made up of two large log homes with living rooms and a small kitchen and bunks in rooms that flanked a shower house. Most of them took meals at the main house or out under the stars.

"One of the two."

Chelsey rolled her eyes but smirked and climbed the porch steps to the bigger log home. She knocked then turned the knob. "Hello, anyone home?"

Silence.

"Sunday is another day, like Ruben said."

"Ruben owns it and gave us permission to do what we need. So I'm going in." Her satisfaction at the loop-hole lit up her face, and it was the first time he'd seen it since she arrived in Gran Valle.

"Guess I am, too, then."

Chelsey entered the house, and Tack followed. The smell of men out in the heat and dirt for too many hours smacked his senses.

"Don't say hossy-stink," she muttered with a curled upper lip.

"Well, I call it like I see it."

They maneuvered through the quiet bunkhouse. For a bunch of cowboys living here, it was tidy. Needed air freshener, but tidy. They entered a bunkroom. Beds made and clear of clutter. They exited and entered the next bunkroom.

Nothing. No one. Chelsey poked around and frowned. "Let's try the shower house."

They left the bunkhouse and followed the paved side-walk that led to the communal showers. "How about I do this one solo? Just in case it's occupied."

"Yes, do spare my eyes. But if it's all clear, holler."

"Will do," he said and entered the shower house.

Chelsey kicked at dirt and surveyed the area. The sec-ond bunkhouse had yet to be checked. She moseyed to-ward it. It was possible Juan had traveled back to Mexico to mourn with family. Chelsey had always been one for questioning people face-to-face, where she could exam-ine their body language and pull details from inflection and tone of voice at the same time. Many expressions were universal, and she was adept at determining who was lying or withholding truth in interviews, whether or not she was the one conducting the interview.

She climbed the porch steps and knocked. Not bothering to announce herself, she entered the bunkhouse and found the same smells of sweaty leather, liniment and musk. This bunk wasn't quite as straight and clutter-free as the first one. She heard stirring toward the last room on the right.

Hairs rose on her neck, and she unholstered her weapon out of sheer precaution and a gut feeling. Quietly, she turned the knob, holding her breath and praying the hinges wouldn't squeak when she pushed the door open.

Once the door was cracked, she used her boot to toe it farther open. Her breath exhaled unevenly at the eerie silence. Not even a shuffle or scoot. Perhaps her ears had played a trick on her. After everything she'd endured since last night, it wouldn't be far-fetched.

Slipping inside the room, she surveyed the bunks.

The last one by the wall caught her attention.

Juan Garcia lay limp, half his body hanging off the side of the bed and his eyes staring wide and lifelessly at the ceiling. Chelsey shivered and turned for the door to report the disturbing findings to Tack, but a thick, braided leather horse rein snaked around her throat from behind. She elbowed her attacker in the sternum, but the grip remained.

He shoved her into the wall, face-first—her tender cheek screaming in protest from being abused again. Chelsey lost the grip on her gun, and it clattered to the floor. Eyes watering and throat burning, she pitched forward, throwing her attacker off balance as the sound of Tack's voice echoed through the bunkhouse.

"Chels, you in here?" he called. "Juan's not in the shower house. It's all clear."

She opened her mouth to cry for help, but her airway was cut off with amazing force, then she heard the buzzing and felt the shock as the taser stunned her once again. She crumpled to the floor, giving him the clear shot to quietly exit the room.

Incapacitated and unable to draw attention to the killer's position, she lay on the wooden floor until the shock stopped racing through her system. By the time Tack entered the room, she was on her hands and knees, gulping in air. "Chels!" He dropped beside her and examined her neck, then sprang up and shot out the door after the Outlaw.

She called 911, then rushed outside. Scanning the property, she saw nothing. No sign of Tack or the Outlaw. She rubbed her side, feeling the soreness of yet another encounter with fifty-thousand volts.

Out of the brush about twenty feet away, Tack jogged toward her, then picked up his pace when he spotted her. "Running in boots is for the birds," he said and gently cupped her shoulders. "You hurt?"

She raised the other side of her shirt, revealing the marks. If Tack hadn't been nearby, she might be inside the bunkhouse in the same condition as Juan.

He lightly touched the seared mark from the stun gun. "I'm going to make sure this guy feels the extent of the law when I get my hands on him."

"Me, too." She lowered her shirt. "Juan is dead, if you didn't notice." As she told him what had happened, they entered the now crime scene, studying it differently. "Juan said Izzy saw her attacker. We thought he was lying, but now that he's dead... I don't think he was."

Chelsey had suspected Juan of deception and possible involvement, and now it appeared the Outlaw was tying up loose ends. "He used the word *told*, and I assumed speaking, but I wonder if she told him in gestures. Nothing written has been found."

"Unless the Outlaw took the incriminating proof with him after killing Izzy."

That's what had marred her profile of the mass shooter in Dallas. No more assuming. "We'll never know now for sure. He's two steps ahead of us."

Tack grimaced and inspected Juan's body. "Same impression on his neck from the braided rein." He glanced at Chelsey and frowned. "Same as on yours. You see him? Was he wearing the bandanna around his face? Cowboy hat?"

"Definitely cowboy hat, and the same one—or at least same color—as last night. I caught a glimpse. But he attacked me from behind, and before I could see his face, he nailed me with the prod, so I can't be certain."

Tack returned to her, tipped up her chin and lightly ran his thumb across the patterns on her neck, sending a new wave of chill bumps on her arms. But this had nothing to do with fear. There was, however, a warning signal. "You need a doctor?" He brushed a strand of hair from her cheek, caressing it. "Tell me what you need, Chelsey," he whispered.

What she needed was distance between them. To remind herself that the feelings warning her to back up were in place for a reason.

But what she wanted was to lean into his words. Lean into his touch. His nearness.

"I'm fine." She retreated a step, and he dropped his hand from her face. "You had perfect timing."

"Good timing. Not perfect."

She grinned, and the crunching of gravel caught her attention. "Here we go again," she muttered.

After they met the deputies and the coroner out front and received gloves, they reentered the bunkhouse. Tack called the Rangers' forensic team, since he had jurisdiction and the murder connected to his cold cases.

"No one locks the bunkhouses. Anyone could have entered, but how did this guy get on and off the property?" Tack asked as he surveyed the door and windows in the living area.

"Hidden vehicle? Horse stashed somewhere? He was in a white Ford last night." Chelsey squatted and examined Juan and what was nearby. Without plate numbers, it would be hard to track a white Ford truck in Texas. "I don't see signs of a struggle. If Izzy told him who had attacked her and Juan knew him, too, there would have been a struggle if he'd seen him coming."

"Let's scope out Izzy's cabin. See if we find any evidence of a boyfriend or some idea of who she was. Where she went."

Victimology was key.

They walked the two hundred feet to Izzy's cabin, surveying the brush and discussing ways to get in and out of the property. "There are several entrances with acreage this large," Tack said. "Plenty of places to stash vehicles, ATVs or even horses. We know he wasn't planning to abduct him or bury him at Big Bend. Only women have been buried there. This was collateral damage, I'm afraid."

Chelsey feared she was collateral damage, too. The Outlaw couldn't be sure of what she'd seen or would remember. He hadn't expected them today, though.

The thought of him being on the property sent a shiver through her bones.

Izzy's cabin was up ahead. Less than a thousand square feet. Older. But perfect for a young woman here on a temporary work visa. The door was unlocked, and they stepped inside, the hints of recently cooked spices lingering along with a flowery scent. Izzy's scent. Could be shampoo or a lotion. An eerie silence hung in the air, and Chelsey frowned. "I never have liked combing the home of a deceased person. I know they're not here, but it feels like an invasion of privacy."

"In the end, it helps us find their perpetrators."

"I know. It's just...odd. I'll take the bedroom and bathroom while you snoop in the living room and kitchen." Chelsey made her way down a narrow hall. One bathroom on the left then a bedroom adjacent. Flipping on the light, she riffled through the small bottom sink cabinet and pulled back the cheap plastic shower curtain. She spotted the source of Izzy's flowery scent—body wash. After rummaging around in the bathroom, she entered the master bedroom. A full-size bed with a deep red comforter. Nothing expensive. One four-drawer dresser was full of worn medium T-shirts. Chelsey went through each drawer and then the closet.

Inside the closet, on the floor, a silver Big Bend pin caught her eye. She stooped, snapped a few photos with her cell phone, then moved a piece of laundry out of the way. "Hey, Tack! I may have something."

Tack entered the room.

"Can you hand me an evidence bag?"

Tack handed her a plastic evidence bag provided by the deputies at the earlier scene. "Why? Is it something notable?"

"Women don't usually wear pins unless it's on a hat or tucked on a purse strap—neither of which are in the closet. It's possible it was given to her as a gift or someone else was wearing it and it came off when the shirt was tossed in the hamper."

"A man?"

"I think so. I don't see any men's shirts, but she could have washed it and given it back and missed the pin. It was tucked into the carpet behind the laundry basket. I can't tell if it's novelty or part of a uniform. Do you know?"

She handed him the bag with the pin, and he studied it. "I'm not sure. But it gives us a place to start looking, though it's going to be like a needle in a haystack. Big Bend National Park is over eight hundred acres total. Several communities host a crew of amenities. Not to mention all the park rangers, Border Patrol. We're combing the desert for a pin."

"Not up to the challenge?" she nudged, sparking his competitive side.

"I didn't say that." There was the fiery Tack she knew well. "I'll get a Ranger analyst on it. Have them search online and try and home in on who wears it or if it's a novelty and how many shops carry it. In the meantime, we need to update the Reddington family, then we can head to the burial site at Big Bend. I'll call Jerry Allen— my connection at the park. Have him meet us out there."

"I like that plan. I haven't been to Big Bend since last time I visited you."

"That was two years ago."

Two years ago, for four days. She'd helped the El Paso PD build a profile on a bank robber ring. They'd caught them thanks to the profile. She'd spent a couple of days with Tack, canoeing the Rio Grande. One night they'd camped out. That long weekend might be the most relaxing she'd done.

"You know, if we're going to drive the hour and a half to get there, we might as well make a Sunday of it. We can talk turkey while we canoe. Take the short ten-mile scenic tour at Mariscal Canyon. We can't talk with your forensic anthropologist for all that face jazz and bone stuff until tomorrow."

Chelsey laughed at Tack's lack of proper definitions. "You need a glossary of some sort. Maybe when she arrives, let me do the talking. One of us needs some semblance of intelligence."

"Key word here, pal, is semblance."

"Do you even know what that means?"

Tack winked. "It means you're as clueless as the next person. You fake it real good, though."

That hit a sour note in this melodic banter between them. She was a fake for sure. Did that best. She held her smile but felt the warmth leave her eyes. "All right, I'm in for a relaxing afternoon." Come Monday morning, it was going to be rocket speed, more sleepless nights and mental fatigue. Law enforcement wasn't for the faint of heart or weak stomachs. It was grueling, not glamourous and often thankless. She didn't even want to get started on the pay scale.

After breaking the news to the Reddington family about Juan, packing bags and changing into hiking gear, they set off for Big Bend National Park. Tack had called Jerry Allen, and Chelsey had texted Charlotte to let her know they'd meet her first thing in the morning at the university and the remains would be logged and transferred to the university lab.

Tack cranked up the radio to country pop, but Chelsey didn't feel upbeat. A storm cloud hung over her chest, heavy and ominous. The tight ball in her gut warned her that at any moment it would open up and rain down terror.

SIX

The narrow gravel road to the park rangers' station had been bumpy and miserable. Sweat rolled down Tack's neck as the sun withered them. Chelsey had gathered her hair in a sloppy knot on her head, a few stray hairs sticking to her neck, but she'd remained relatively quiet as she observed the sights. All work at the moment. No pleasure.

Jerry Allen had been happy to meet them and drive them to the camping areas on the dirt road, but the burial site was about fifty yards west of the campgrounds. Off the grid. No bikes. Only feet. Jerry stopped and used his hankie to wipe his forehead. Former military and built like a fortress, Jerry could easily pass for ten years younger than his forty-five years. "What I want to know is how he hauled a dead body up through this."

Tack sighed and sipped from his water bottle. The climb was steady with desert succulents and brush claiming the land they had to push through. The Rio Grande below with the Chisos Mountains flanking it was a beautiful sight, but someone had desecrated the beauty, wrecking lives then burying his secrets along this view.

"He's strong. I can attest. And he's doing it with the sun down and a reprieve from the heat. He could squeeze a dolly up here, but that's a stretch. He'd have had proper gear, equipment, lighting. Time was on his side, and he knew it. Knows it." Chelsey removed her sunglasses and shielded her eyes with her hands. "This spot means something to him. Of all the entrances, I find it hard to believe this was the easiest, most convenient area. It's personal."

She knelt and studied the ground. "Not traveled. But it is a gorgeous view. Like being on top of the world." Her eyes clouded and Tack knew she was going deep into her zone, not paying attention to him or Jerry. Her own little profiling world. "Maybe that's it. Secluded but a feeling of being king. This is his outdoor castle. A palace of trophies. A mountain of victory. No one knows his secrets. No one ever would have—until the couple with the dog decided to get nosy and the dog decided to dig." She shook out of her thoughts, almost appearing startled she'd been in it. "I can't believe someone would sneak a pet into the park. It's dumb and dangerous."

"Couple's name is Turner. Lola and Payton. Mid-twenties." They'd gotten more than they bargained for veering off the proper path. Man, that would preach.

"I want to talk to them." She stood and eyed Jerry. "How often is this area patrolled?"

"Rarely to never. We keep rangers on trails and near campgrounds and rivers. There is no way to manpower all of Big Bend on a daily or routine basis—that is, the areas outside the rules." Jerry slurped from his bottle of water and wiped his lips. "The graves are up ahead."

They followed Jerry a few more feet northeast. Crime scene tape had been removed, but the open graves remained. "You get dogs up here, see if they could sniff out more bodies?"

"And ground-penetrating radar. Chemical analysis of soil and air. Within one hundred feet. Nothing but what we got," Tack said, working not to be irritated with Chelsey. He knew how to do his job, but she was in the zone and not taking any of that into consideration.

The graves were about eight feet apart, forming a circle. "I wonder if this means anything. I'd like to see the photos. See if they're buried with their toes in the center of the circle or their heads. Meticulous placing will also mean something to him."

"I have photos on my phone." He'd kept files and the pictures to refer to often. He pulled them up and cupped his hand over the screen to shade the photos for Chelsey. "Heads are placed toward the inner circle and feet out."

"Like they're lying down looking out at the mountains," Chelsey noted. "Interesting. I wish we knew when they were buried. Maybe it's significant. Was it on a night when there was a full moon? If so, he might have brought them up here to lie and stare up at it—romantic."

Tack curled his upper lip. Chelsey had to go to the most depraved ideas because her job generally took her to those places. Serial killers weren't kind, clean and pure. They were sick and void of humanity and mercy.

"That's creepy," Jerry said.

"Agreed," Chelsey said and dusted her hands on her khaki cargo pants. Sighing, she cocked her head. "Jerry, you know where this pin might come from?" She retrieved her cell phone and scrolled to the photo and showed him the pin they'd found in Izzy's closet. "Novelty item? Worn by an official or park ranger?"

Jerry studied the photo. "Yeah, I recognize it. Worn

by Big Bend Adventure Tour Guides. They provide shuttles to Big Bend as well as local hiking tours and river guides. This is one of theirs."

Chelsey looked at Tack. "Izzy could have completed a tour, but I didn't see her so much of a tourist as a hard worker who took her job seriously."

"Well, she clearly had leisure time. Whether she did a guided tour or had a tour guide as a friend." Or more. "At least we have a jumping-off point. Someone with the company might recognize her."

Unless he was the killer and wanted to remain hidden.

Maybe they could catch a break and get a print from the pin. Chelsey took a few photos with her phone, and they trekked back to the dirt road and climbed into Jerry's Bronco. Back down the mountain, jostling and bouncing, they made it to the ranger station and left Jerry.

"How do you feel about canoeing?"

"I feel like I could use some cool water on my skin. I want some time to roll over what I saw in my brain. I need a cup of ice."

Tack hooted. "Yeah, that will last two seconds before it's water." They climbed into his truck and drove about thirty minutes to Talley Ranch Road. Tack unloaded the canoe from his truck while Chelsey hauled gear and life vests from the back seat.

"You got the permits, right?"

"Yes, and we're all good for a shuttle to take us back to the truck once we end in Solis."

"Okay." She grinned. "Just checking. Hope you don't get broken into. Vandalism on backcountry is nuts."

Once they had everything secured, they hauled the canoe into the water, the cool drops relieving his skin from the heat. Chelsey dipped her hand in then splashed her neck. "Heave ho, bro."

Tack chortled. "Steer left. It won't be far before we hit—"

"Rock Pile Rapid. I know. Last thing we need is getting hung up in trees and debris that have floated down here." They began their journey down the Rio Grande as it dipped down between the Mariscal's limestone cliffs rising up to fourteen hundred feet, glistening in the sun like tiny diamonds tucked into the red, earthy-colored rock.

"How can anyone not believe in God when gazing on this?" It was incredible. Breathtaking.

"I don't know," she murmured as they rowed in unison, making a smooth and solid partnership. The river was quiet sans the stirring water. Green jays swooped and fluttered around the canyons, their green bodies contrasting with their bright blue-and-black heads. "Hey, maybe it'll be our day. Rarely see green jays."

Chelsey grunted her answer.

Up ahead, a huge boulder jutted from the river, and Tack felt Chelsey direct the canoe to the left; he evened her out as they steered to that side of the boulder to keep from being caught.

Only ten miles of water, but the scenery felt unending. This was the place to relax.

They passed the boulder and debris. "I really need Charlotte to come through for us on identifying the other victims. I'd like to know where they worked, who they knew—particularly if they knew someone from a local tour guide company. All we have to go on is Izzy and Rosa. Did you find out if Rosa had a boyfriend or visited Big Bend? Maybe the killer gave a pin to all his victims."

So much for relaxing. Tack lifted the oar from the water, letting the canoe glide forward with the current. About half a mile down, they'd have to work through the first good rapid at the Tight Squeeze—a flat block of stone covering the riverbed. "She had two friends she knew from the Sparkling Bend Ranch, where she worked. Both said she enjoyed exploring and had a male friend she accompanied, but they didn't think it was romantic in nature. I sensed some hesitation, though."

"Maybe they're afraid to talk to a man. Don't trust men. I might be able to get through. Get answers."

"We'll add it to our to-do list tomorrow. Gonna be long days. Long nights."

"Yep." She inhaled. "Here we go," she said.

Tight Squeeze, a narrow, shallow channel, came into view. "Let's run and end hard left, avoid the boulder. Like last time." Best to get a game plan. This was the first significant current, and they had about a three-foot drop coming.

"On it."

The currents increased, moving them forward as the rushing water picked up pace, but he and Chelsey had rowed before. They had this. He hoped.

No time to enjoy the canyon yet. Tack concentrated on getting through the first rapid. A few canoes and tents were perched on the edge of the canyon—no people noticeable, though. As the channel narrowed, they maneuvered the canoe forward, bouncing as if on air.

Dots of water sprayed and splashed Tack's arms. Chelsey squealed at the cold water and giggled. "Heave—"

Her words died on her lips as the gun blast echoed

on the canyon walls and water sprayed from the bullet entering the river at the back.

"Where's it coming from?" Chelsey screeched. Jagged boulders jutted from the water. Cliffs and caves surrounded them. Fast rapid. Could they bail into the water and remain unscathed?

No way he played it that they came out without injury or fatality.

Another projectile hit the edge of the canoe, spraying bits of wood and overlay.

"Do we jump?" Chelsey shrieked as the canoe jostled in the water. They were going in the river either way if they didn't get control, and it was nearly impossible to concentrate on rowing in open water with a shooter following them through the cliffs above.

Tight Squeeze wasn't long before it opened back up into quieter waters. If they could row through it without being used as target practice, they might have a chance of jumping ship and hiding in a crag or cave on the other side of the canyon. But they'd lose their canoe.

Chelsey shrieked and tumbled over the side of the canoe.

"Chelsey!"

Icy water invaded Chelsey's mouth, rushing down her throat and cutting off precious air. Her life vest thrust her above the surface as she coughed and sputtered, her lungs burning. "Tack," she choked out. Arms flailing, she had to gain control of her faculties.

Panic tempted to override calm thoughts. Everything was moving so fast and chaotically. Her pulse spiked, but she forced herself to think logically, clearly and rationally or she'd drown, but seeing dozens of jagged rocks jutting from the flatbed and knowing a hidden shooter lay somewhere in the crags above worked her heart rate over.

Another projectile hit the water near the rock beside her, and she shrieked, her preserver keeping her from ducking underwater.

"Tack!"

A firm, large grip took hold of her hand. "Chelsey, I can't bring you back into the canoe, hon."

What?

Suddenly, Tack dived into the water with her, never releasing his grip. He was with her. He hadn't left her. Relief only lasted briefly before the shooter rained more bullets. The water yanked and dragged them farther down the river. Chelsey's shoulder wrenched against a limestone rock, and she cried out.

"We have to get to ground. Stay with me." He looped her hand through his life vest to help her keep ahold of him. "I need both my hands. You hang on." His hair had flattened to his head, water ran in rivulets down his face, but his gaze was steady. Centered.

He kept one hand on the canoe, but his biceps convulsed, and the vein in his neck protruded. How long could he tame the now makeshift shield, keep them both from crashing upon the rocks and guide them safely into quieter waters ahead?

Chelsey grabbed an edge of the upturned canoe and worked her feet to partner with Tack, but terror nipped at her faculties. If she didn't focus, it would devour her sound mind and easily steal their lives, whether by gunfire or impaling themselves on a boulder.

"Once we get through Tight Squeeze, we'll have other options," Tack said in a clipped tone.

"What options?" She didn't see any. The shooter could continue along the canyon walls, remain in hiding and easily pick them off. Ironically, the only saving grace they had at the moment was the challenging rapids and the maze of boulders. Once the water settled and softened, the shooter might not miss.

Tack grimaced, and Chelsey knew a rock had collided with his body. They'd be banged and bloodied and bruised for days if they made it out alive. The canoe clanged against a gargantuan rock, and Tack lost his grip but quickly regained it. "Okay, we're going to have to lose the canoe. We can go faster without it. Once we get to the slower rapids, we'll climb up into the crags on the other side."

"Okay," she said as she slammed into a boulder, losing her breath with the jolt.

"Move in front of me. Wrap your arms around my neck and your legs around my waist."

A bullet slammed into the rocks above them. The shots weren't being fired as rapidly now, but only because the current was moving them faster than the killer could climb and scramble over mountain terrain.

"I can shield you from the guy with the gun and the rocks."

"You don't need to shield me," she said through pants and the throbbing ache sweeping through her bones. "I can handle it."

"No, you can't. I love you, honey, but you're not as strong as me. One more crash and I could lose you. And I'm not losing you. Not now. Not ever. Now, be a good girl and do what I ask."

She coughed and slid in front of him, facing him. "If I put my arms around your neck, you can't see."

"You let me worry about that." His voice was commanding but soft. She briefly peered into his eyes, lashes dotted with river water. He wasn't simply brave. Wasn't throwing out empty promises or words. He meant what he was saying. Tack would keep them safe, and she fully believed him. Willingly, she wrapped her arms around his neck and slid her legs around his waist. Her nose brushed his, and he had the audacity, in a time like this, to grin.

And that's when she knew they were coming out of this river.

Certainly not unscathed. Certainly not without her heart rate spiking to dangerous levels. But he would make sure the waters didn't claim her.

Bullets might get them. But the rocks and water would not take her.

She wasn't sure when her cheek rested against his, when her grasp around him tightened, but then the waters quieted, the current ebbed.

And the atmosphere became silent.

Tack leaned backward and kicked his legs toward the bank. He scraped matted hair off her face and kissed her forehead. "You okay?"

At the cool touch of his lips on her skin, her pulse kicked up another notch.

She was safe from the waters taking her under, but she was far from safe when it came to being drowned in Tack's goodness, his protectiveness, his pure masculinity. The only thing she had keeping her afloat was the secret she harbored.

Tack's brow met hers, resting, as his breaths came in heavy puffs.

"Yes." As fine as she could be. "You?"

He pulled away and heaved a sigh. "That was worse than breaking a bronc. Shots have dwindled. But I don't think we're out of the woods yet."

"I wish we were running in woods. I feel so…vulnerable out here."

He tipped her chin. "You don't think I can get you the rest of the way," he whispered.

"I know you can." That's what terrified her most—how much she depended on him and how deeply she knew and trusted him. "But you look like you want to sit here on this rock and kiss me." She chose light-hearted teasing to break the moment and dull the zing and awareness between them.

"Wouldn't that be straight out of a romance." He tucked a wet strand of hair behind her ear.

"Yeah, but in real life, the killer isn't going to wait a beat to allow us time to get all smoochy."

"You're right. And we've been there, done that once before anyway." He hauled her up to her feet.

"True. Like kissing my brother." Except it hadn't been repulsive in the slightest. That one summer night. Heat licking at her skin, the sun setting behind the mountains. And Tack's impressive lips testing hers. Could they be more? Should they be?

"We're going to have to climb our way up. I see a crevice that leads into a cave. We may have to hang out awhile. And you don't have a brother," he retorted as he led her behind a large rock that would shield the beginning of their ascent up the canyon. "You go first. The rocks are large enough to grasp and stand on. Just be careful. Your feet are wet. No slipping."

No slipping.

She grabbed the rough and gritty limestone, then

began climbing. About twenty feet up, a meager ledge with a large crevice beckoned them.

"I'm right behind you. Keep going."

Sweat trickled down her heated cheeks and her hands turned clammy, but she kept hunting for the right rock to cling to, one that would give her sure footing for the climb. The sounds of gravel coming loose and slipping reminded her that Tack was behind her, watching to make sure her footing stayed firm. And if she did stumble, she had full trust he'd keep her from falling.

Chelsey refused to depend on Tack like this. It wasn't fair to either of them. She'd learned long ago to be independent and rely on herself. This was too intense. Too… too…revealing. "Don't do any profiling down there, if you get my drift," she said with a light tone she wasn't feeling.

A killer was tracking them. She'd never felt more somber and serious. But then her heart decided to perk up and cast a few unwanted feelings in her fevered face.

Of all the audacity. Now? At a time like this? When she couldn't guard her heart or take measured control of her thoughts. It was flat out rude on her heart's part.

Tack's husky chuckle reached her ears. "Never, ever would I do anything less than gentlemanly."

"So you say," she muttered as she stretched upward for the next rock to grab onto. Her foot slid against the stone, and she lost her footing. As she yelped, her hand released the rock and she flailed backward, but Tack caught her with his left arm.

"What did I tell you about being careful?"

She held his gaze, then felt his muscles straining under the pressure to hold her upright and keep them both secure on the canyon wall.

"I slipped." Just like with the profile. But no one had caught her. She'd fallen and run. Run straight to the man holding her up now.

Regaining her ground and grip, she pushed herself onto the ledge, small pebbles biting into her palms, covering her with dust. Tack climbed up behind her.

"We made it."

Gunfire erupted.

Tack cried out.

SEVEN

Pressure and a sting tore into Tack's left shoulder, the closest shoulder to Chelsey. The life vest had protected him somewhat. "I'm grazed. Fine. You're the target. Inside the crevice. Now!"

Chelsey scrambled, wide-eyed and red faced. They hustled into the darkness of cover. Large enough for them to stand hunched. "How far back do you think this leads?" Chelsey asked.

"I don't know. It might be part of Hermit's Cave. Can't say for sure." He winced at the burning wound. "And we're not equipped to spelunk."

They had no weapons, no supplies. Not even a flashlight. The darkness lingering in the cave was impenetrable. Almost tangible.

"We do need to get against the walls. In case he blindly fires inside." Tack guided Chelsey farther back and against the cool rock wall. Next to him, she shuddered. "You cold?"

"I hate the dark, and more than that…scorpions. You think there's scorpions in here, Tackitt?" she asked with a tremor in her voice. A gunman was outside and she'd braved it like a champ, though he wasn't unaware of her schemes to mask the fear, to bring the tension levels down using easy banter with a hint of flirting. But reminding him of that one kiss they'd shared in their teenage years had put her lips on his brain. Had somewhat helped him keep his mind off being blindsided and shot in the shoulder by a gunman.

She might not have been into the kiss. Although, if memory served, she'd been rather gung-ho. Or maybe he'd imagined it—romanticized the event. And to him, it had been an event. Chelsey had broken the kiss, and he'd spotted the flash of fear before she'd laughed and played it off as too friendly. Hadn't felt friendly to him.

"Tack, I mean it. Don't lie. What are the chances of getting stung by venomous scorpions?"

"Greater than getting popped by a bullet."

She groaned. "Okay, I changed my mind. Lie to me."

Tack drew her to his side, flinching at his wounded shoulder.

"How bad it is? Can you tell?" she asked.

"I don't think it's fatal. Be nice to see it, though." In blackness like this, there was no chance of their eyes adjusting. She leaned against him. "You'll be fine. Scorpions are nocturnal. They're snug as a bug."

"As long as my sock isn't the rug, I'm fine."

He laid his cheek on the top of her damp head. "We need a game plan."

If the gunman had provisions, he could wait them out easily, knowing they had nothing, not even a bottle of water to quench their parched throats, and Tack's throat was desert dry. He could be working his way to the cave, but if he was smart—and they knew he was—he'd realize they could be gone by the time he made it around the canyon wall to their side. But how much time did they let pass before going out into the open?

Time eked by as they waited with bated breath. "Tack?" she whispered unnecessarily. The shooter wouldn't hear them. No one would.

"Yeah."

"I'm sorry you got stuck in a cave with me because a homicidal maniac wants me dead. This was supposed to be a relaxing afternoon." The regret and remorse in her voice tucked itself deep inside him, and he drew her closer. She rested her head on his life vest, which they still wore in case they needed to jump back into the river.

"You know what, Chels? Cave. River. Doesn't matter to me. I'm just glad to see you alive. And that's how I'm gonna keep you." No matter what it cost. Losing Chelsey would bring a tsunami of grief, and he'd never recover. He wasn't strong enough. She'd been his friend for too long. His confidante. His source of joy over the years. When he and Tamera Verde broke up the day before prom, Chelsey had dropped her date and stood in for Tamera. Her date likely hadn't gotten over it.

Tack had begged her to not bail, but she didn't have anything romantic cooking with Javier Dominguez. Her dress hadn't matched Tack's tux and vest. But that hadn't stopped them from dancing the night away. Hadn't stopped her from helping him over the sore heart Tamera had stomped on. But that had only been a crush. Because by an hour in, Tack had forgotten about Tamera.

"Remember my senior prom?"

"Ah. Tamera what's-her-name broke your heart."

"No, she didn't. I only thought she had." He sighed. "You've always been there for me. I plan to be here for you. So in your own words from that long-ago debacle, 'Shut your fat mouth and let me be your best friend.'"

Chelsey giggled. "I do have a way with words."

Tack kissed the top of her head. A gesture he'd done often for as long as he could remember, but something about it now and earlier on the rocky shore when he'd kissed her brow…it felt different. He'd been relieved they'd made it onto the solid rock. But the kiss might have been more than simply relief. More than habit. Or maybe not. He couldn't go there, explore it further.

"Actually it was my *words* that landed us here. And possibly put me in danger with whoever actually killed all those women in Dallas."

"Don't start getting discouraged now. I need your sassy self. She's the one who's gonna help us down this mountain and to the shuttle. To safety. And bring me comedic relief when I want to spit nails."

"Okay, shutting my fat mouth right now."

"I'm going to test the opening. It's the only way. We've been in here a while." Though it was hard to gauge timing when suspense was killing them. Could have been ten minutes even if it felt like an hour. Tack couldn't be sure.

She grabbed his arm as he pulled away. "You need to know, in case it gets ugly, I love you, Tackitt."

Over the years, she'd said it thousands of times. So had he. He did love Chelsey. Had always felt protective over her. But hearing it now, in this setting, it shifted little pebbles of emotion that had settled in his chest. Stirred them up, creating a dust of feelings he would have preferred to remain settled at the murky bottom of his heart.

"I love you, too, but nothing is going to happen."

She released her grip on his arm, and he maneuvered to the lip of the cave. Now or never. Bracing himself, he stepped out, the sunlight blinding him. He covered his eyes and squinted. "I think he gave up," Tack called.

Suddenly, Chelsey was at the mouth of the cave, mimicking him with her hand over her blinded eyes. "No. He's not after you. He'd be waiting on me." She stepped out at his protest, but sadly she was right.

She stood in the open on the ledge of the mountain. Waiting. Tack's pulse ratcheted. After a few moments, he nodded. "We have to try."

It was possible he was still there and waiting for them to move farther into the open area with no cave to retreat to. But it was a risk they had to take.

"I'm going first. Stay behind me. I'll shield you. In case…"

"In case he's waiting and luring me out. Yeah, I've already thought of that." Chelsey kept to his back, and they eased their way around the ledge. No ropes to secure them. He glanced down, and his head spun. But the canoe was long gone down the river, and they couldn't swim that far or take their chances and hope other rafters would find them.

Tack paused. "Go in front again if we're going to climb upward. I can catch you."

"Yeah, well, who's shielding you and catching your fall?" she asked but slowly moved around him. The cliff's edge was only about two feet wide in most places, and narrower in others. His nerves buzzed as Chelsey started the ascent. If they could climb up about five feet, they'd be able to use the canyon's naturally cut trail— and he was using that term loosely—to get to Solis, where the river tour ended and the shuttles were waiting to return tourists to their vehicles.

The sun baked their skin regardless of the sunscreen they'd slathered on before the trip. Chelsey stretched her arms, clinging to rocks that had heated along with the temperature. Before long, they might be too hot to touch.

That presented a brand-new issue. One he didn't want to ponder. "Take your time, but hurry up," he said.

Chelsey responded with an incoherent mutter. A canyon wren soared beside them, and Chelsey flinched, losing her grip as her foot slid off the rock she'd been bracing herself on. She shrieked and slid down. Tack gripped his rock, securing himself, and jutted out his hip and leg to break her fall. Her impact pushed him backward and he lost some of his ground; his heart lurched into his throat, and his breathing came in pants as a sandpiper wheeted nearby.

"You good?" he asked, not even attempting to mask his fear. That was too close.

"Yeah." The tremors in her voice and hands said otherwise. She sucked in air as she regained her footing and latched on to the rock above, hoisting herself up. Tack followed her path, and they worked steadily, climbing up and over, repeat. Sweat poured down his back, sticking his T-shirt to his skin, and dripped from the tip of his nose as he continued to stretch and stagger between the rocks.

They finally reached the end of the course, and Chelsey collapsed on her back in the desert, the neck of her shirt laden with sweat and her hair stuck to her damp neck and red cheeks. Dirt stained her face and bare arms.

Neither of them spoke as they rested and worked

to catch their breath. Tack wasn't out of shape by any means, but that was no joke.

"Remind me to never, ever agree to go on a canoe trip with you. Tell me you have your keys," she said and sat up, dirt now clinging to the back of her shirt.

He'd left his Glock, wallet and phone—no point bringing it with spotty to no cell service in the park—in the truck. He hadn't wanted to tip the canoe and lose anything, not to mention he hadn't expected to be followed and attacked. But he'd kept the keys. He held them up and shook them.

"Music to my ears, Tackitt. I don't know if I can get back up and move another step. Carry me," she said with a slight smirk.

"Honey, if I could, I would. But I don't know if I can pick myself up." He held out his grimy hand, and she placed her equally grimy one in his. He hauled her to her feet and rustled her messy bun on her head. "When we catch this guy, I'm gonna throw him off that canyon."

Chelsey laughed at his teasing. "No, you're not."

"No?"

"Because I'm gonna do it."

Tack sighed, and they slipped into easy banter as they waited for the shuttle, then made it to his truck. But they were on edge. Chelsey had moved slowly, but her eyes had been roaming like an eagle. Tack had been wary of the few people who had been on the shuttle or walking on the backcountry. They didn't know who the Outlaw was or if it was even him who had shot at them. Might have been the mass shooter since he liked guns, but the way this guy had known the canyons seemed like someone with more local knowledge. Tack wasn't taking any chances regardless. Not with Chelsey's life.

* * *

Chelsey's entire body ached. After leaving Solis, they drove straight to a convenience store and bought bottles of water, draining them dry then ordering greasy fried chicken tenders and a score of potato logs from a nearby fast food joint.

She ached to rid the grime and this day from her skin and crawl into soft sheets. Checking her phone, she saw two missed calls from Dad. Another round of nervous stomach began.

Dad had no clue she was in Texas. Guilt nipped at her for avoiding his calls. He never asked her for anything—not even participation in whatever new con he was cooking up—but the tension was there like an invisible wall. She wasn't in a mental state to deal with him, though his calls were always upbeat and positive. Generally focused on her and her career. Words of encouragement and how proud he was of her.

But she wasn't proud of him. Or herself.

She tucked the phone back in her purse and relished the air-conditioning vent blasting sweet cool air on her sticky face. Tack had the radio down low. The water had dried and his wavy curls were unruly, like a little boy after waking from a nap. Usually they were combed back and as in control as he was.

"Shooter had to be somewhat familiar with the lay of the land. Keeping on the US side of the canyon and knowing how to hide himself. More and more I'm thinking someone from a tour guide company."

"We'll visit Big Bend Adventure Tour Guides tomorrow after we meet with your forensic anthropologist friend—"

"Charlotte."

"Charlotte," he mimicked. "Then swing by River Valley Bend, where Rosa Velasquez worked, and talk to her employers—Brick and Donna Saget. Go from there."

Chelsey agreed with his plan. They turned on the dirt road leading to Redd Rock Ranch where Chelsey was staying, drove up and through the gate to the driveway. It was quiet this late. Chelsey noticed a bubble mailer on the front porch. She clambered from the truck, her muscles sore and stiff, but her mind on full alert, her pulse increasing as she approached the package.

She knelt. "Can you get me a pair of latex gloves from your truck?"

"You sure you should mess with it?"

"No." She wasn't sure of anything. Tack brought her gloves and reluctantly handed them to her. She picked up the small gold envelope. Whatever was inside was lightweight. Postmark from Dallas. No return address. "It's from him. The real mass shooter."

"How about you open it out here, just in case."

Chelsey carefully opened the envelope. Inside was a hot-pink T-shirt with the gym's logo. On the back of the shirt it read, In Memory Of, then listed the names of every woman who had died inside the gym that morning.

The T-shirt was accompanied by a note.

Agent Banks,
  All that justice served was in vain. How will the families feel when they find out the man who took away their precious little calves is still out there and the best of the best is nothing but a phony? Will your apologies for mucking it all up be enough?
  I highly doubt it.

PS Still no news. Keeping secrets? Can't keep them for long.

Tack took the letter encased in the clear plastic bag and frowned. "What's this guy's goal?"

Chelsey would like to know the same. "Two of my colleagues are looking into the case, but so far they haven't sent me any new information or a more solid profile."

The mass shooter's taunts should slough off like water on a duck's back, but she was allowing each word to sink her and solidify what she already knew to be true. It was like this guy was privy to her past. A deathly cold chill slithered down her spine. What if he was? How hard would it be to dig until something popped? No. Dad had never been to prison. Never been charged. He'd been careful. Even Chelsey had struggled to find what she needed to prove what he'd done to Tack's family.

She leaned over Tack's arm and read the letter again. "That's twice now," she murmured.

"Twice what?"

"He's used ranch jargon. In the first letter, he used the term *ranny* when talking about me being a terrible leader or person in charge. Now he's referring to the shooting victims as calves."

"You think he's one and the same as the Outlaw?" Skepticism slanted his eyebrows.

"No. I'm not sure if he wants to drive home the fact he knows exactly where I am right now. Not just a physical location, but an actual ranch, as if he's watching. Or he's familiar with ranches and maybe grew up on one. Might work a ranch."

"So he's either including a few ranch terms deliberately or it's ingrained in his vocabulary and he doesn't realize it."

"One of the two." She nodded. "And if it's the latter, he's making mistakes. We can work with linguistics. Narrow down where he might be or have come from. We know he purchased a memorial T-shirt."

"Probably in cash."

"It's worth asking the new manager to release online buyers' purchase information and receipts for those who bought a shirt in person."

First thing in the morning. One more item to add to their mountainous list.

Monday morning came, and Chelsey's body ached. Getting out of bed had been something straight out of a Frankenstein movie—every muscle stiff and screaming in agony, but the hot water from the shower had helped loosen them up, and makeup had been a lifeline for covering abrasions and bruises. Lip pencil had erased most of the evidence of a split lip.

She'd donned lightweight khaki slacks with a matching blazer and a simple white shirt underneath. After braiding her hair and coiling it in a knot at the base of her neck, she'd selected sensible shoes.

Tack hadn't said much over breakfast—an egg hash mix he'd rustled up and cooked. He hadn't shied away from the jalapeño peppers, but she'd noticed a bottle of antacid sitting beside his wallet and keys. She might need one herself.

Now, she unbuckled her seat belt at Lonestar State University and slid her credentials into the inner pocket of her summer blazer. The clear blue sky held nothing but the radiant sun. Not a single cloud. It was going to be a scorcher. "Charlotte's already been here since before dawn. Hopefully she'll know some preliminary information that will lend us some help."

Tack nodded and unfolded from the truck. "I didn't sleep at all last night. You?"

Chelsey felt a tug of guilt. She'd known Tack was only down the hall, and that had given her the peace to drift off knowing she was safe. Who had his back? "I did. Maybe you should stop eating such spicy food."

"I'm a Texan. That's like asking sharks to spend more time on land." He hit the fob, and the locks clicked in place with a high-pitched beep.

"Enjoy the chalky antacids, then."

"They're pills. I can't taste 'em," he said with a big, fat dose of smarty-pants.

"Whatever. Your lack of sleep does not justify a cranky attitude today."

He snorted. "Pot, meet kettle."

"I'm not cranky."

"You slept!" He opened the doors to the biology wing, and a rush of frigid air immediately cooled her skin. "But I happen to know you're a grizzly bear when sleep-deprived."

"Well, we're not talking about me," she said matter-of-factly and entered the elevator.

"But there's just so much to say," he mumbled and punched the second-floor button to the labs.

She ignored his snarky banter and exited when the elevator opened. The smells of metal and bleach filled her nose. "That way," she said and pointed to the left end of the hall. The lab was even colder, with stainless steel tables, stools and cooling units. Charlotte stood with her back to them, small in stature. Natural reddish tones to her rich sable hair that was pulled back in a sloppy braid. "Hey," Chelsey said, and Charlotte started and turned, her hooded dark eyes filled with shock, then excitement.

"I'd come hug you but…" She held up two human bones and shrugged. She wore gloves and safety glasses, but it did nothing to mask her classic beauty.

"This is Ranger Tack Holliday. He's working the unsolved homicides I was telling you about."

"Nice to meet you," she said politely, but Chelsey observed the quick dilation of her eyes. Tack was attractive in a rugged, manly way. Charlotte would likely want to study his pheromones or something. She was more into studying men than dating them. "Well, down to business. I've studied the reports and findings from the detectives. I've spent the morning gathering information you probably already know. Young women. Late teens to early twenties. Same bone structure. Your killer likes his prey average height. About five-five to five-six. Petite."

They did already know that. "I was expecting some new initial information or a phone call letting me know there was nothing as of yet."

Charlotte blushed. "Sorry. I was hoping to have something. I should have called."

"No. I'm just cranky. Sorry. You're doing us a huge favor and it is good to see you in person."

"You're welcome." She grinned.

"How long will the reconstruction take?"

"Depends. These women have a lot in common besides Hispanic heritage, so they'll likely look similar in hair and eye color. Dark. I'm going to do a two-dimensional over three. It'll save us time, and it's more cost-effective. I'll figure out the timeline of the murders. See how far back this killer goes—at least with these victims."

"Brilliant. I have a feeling the circle of victims are his only victims—at least in this manner of death. He might have started earlier in life and developed a signature and pattern. We've disrupted his burial ground. He'll have to find a new place. A significant place to him."

"How'd you get into this?" Tack asked Charlotte.

"I've always been a sculptor, an artist. In college I was interested in people. I studied anthropology, and after I finished up my doctorate, I was asked to consult on a case. And that was that." But her tight features didn't match her loose tone. No matter—they weren't here to discuss her personal life. "We should have some good images in about a week. Maybe earlier—if I'm having a bout of insomnia."

Chelsey felt that statement to the core of her being. She had periods of the same suffering. Last night was unusual.

"You have wonderful bone structure," Charlotte said, pointing to Tack's face.

"Uh…thanks?" Tack said.

Charlotte blushed again. "Hazard of my job. Your facial features are symmetrical, the defined jaw…" She studied his face, and Tack frowned.

"You don't want to, like, dip me in acid so you can ogle my bones, do you?"

Charlotte hooted. "No."

"Phew." Tack wiped the back of his hand over his brow. "I was starting to worry," he teased.

"I can ogle your skeletal features without removing skin." She scrunched her nose. "That sounded way too Hannibal Lecter."

"Agreed."

Were they flirting? Ugh. "Time isn't on our side and since you don't have anything, we should be going."

"Right." Tack thanked Charlotte, and they left the university. In the past thirty minutes, the temperature had risen several degrees. The cab of his truck was stuffy and too warm. She shrugged out of her blazer and lightly laid it in the back seat.

"You hit it right off with Charlotte, didn't you?" she asked as she buckled up and Tack reversed from their parking spot.

"She seems smart."

Chelsey rolled her eyes behind her dark sunglasses. "I mean, you know…did you think she was pretty? Did you admire her bone structure?"

He chuckled then frowned. "Are you trying to set me up, while on a case no less?" A hint of irritation traveled through his tone, and his jaw flexed.

"No. I mean… I don't know." Was she? The idea of him getting serious with someone sent an anxious feeling through her gut. Which was selfish. She had no rights to him, no staked claim to his affections, and he deserved happiness. A woman who loved him and wanted to settle down on a little Texas ranch. But that would mean Chelsey would lose the intimate friendship they'd built. It would belong to another. So why was she asking? Pushing? Was she hoping for a particular answer? Might she be simply testing him? That made her feel awful, too.

"I'm a big boy, Chels. I can meet someone and ask them out all on my own. Been doing that awhile now." His words had a bite, as if she'd angered him.

"Sorry. Your love life is yours, and I'm sorry to meddle. It's just Charlotte is such a catch—"

"Chelsey!" Tack sharply cut her off. "I don't want to date Charlotte. I'm not interested in *Charlotte.*" He sighed. "Sorry. I'm—"

"Tired," they said in unison.

Seemed deeper than that. As if he was keeping something—someone—from her. Would he keep a relationship from Chelsey? "I'm sorry, too. Where we heading?"

"Redd Rock's neighboring ranch, where Rosa worked."

"River Valley Bend. Owned by Brick and Donna Saget. What do you know about them?"

Tack flicked his blinker and jumped on US-385 North. "Brick Saget has been in ranching as long as Ruben Reddington. Owns his family's land. Donna is his fourth marriage. Ten years. They have two children together. Eight and ten. Both were oopsies. From what I've heard, Brick has a wandering eye and Donna's pregnancy sealed the marriage deal, then she had the other child a couple years later—also unexpected." His tone sounded skeptical.

"You think she got pregnant to secure the marriage and possibly had baby number two to keep it. Does she have children from other marriages?" Could be a pattern.

"No previous marriages. Just one adult child from a teen pregnancy."

"How long had Rosa worked for them? Any prior nannies we could talk to?"

Tack glanced at her with an amused look. "Plenty. Rosa was their ninth nanny in ten years. I talked with the four I could locate when Rosa went missing."

"Wow. Brick's wandering eye wander to the previous

nannies?" They passed a semitruck on the wrong side, and Chelsey arched an eyebrow.

"They should know to get over."

She said nothing. "How long had Rosa been on staff before she died?"

"Six months."

"You think Brick made any passes at her?"

"I asked him in the last interview. He said no. Donna never mentioned Brick's roving eye. I heard that from a ranch hand."

Why would she bring that up? Humiliation, at the least. Complicit to murder, at best. "I want to see that list of previously employed nannies. Once Charlotte has faces, we might find a pattern—those women could have all worked for the Saget family."

"I'll forward it to you when we get stopped."

Tack hopped off the exit and pulled into a fast food joint drive-through. "You hungry yet?"

"Nope." He rolled his window down, waiting for the attendant to let him know he could order. "I need a large Coke and a large cup of ice, please."

Chelsey grinned, and her insides went warm and fuzzy.

He waggled his eyebrows. "I know you'll be thinking, and we have thirty more minutes of think time." Pulling up to the next window, he paid then approached the second window for his drink and Chelsey's ice. He handed it to her with a knowing grin.

She popped the plastic top off and loaded up on a mouthful, crunching into it. Back on the road, she rolled around theories, but without facts and interviews it wasn't moving anywhere.

The cup was almost empty when they turned down

the long road and drove through the gate at River Valley Bend. The home was less impressive than the Reddingtons' main house. But it was large with floor-to-ceiling windows. Pristine white with green grass and gorgeous landscaping. More luxurious than efficient. They stepped into the heat, and Chelsey inhaled the smell of horses, hay and chlorine. A pool truck was in the circular drive.

Tack took the lead and rang the front doorbell. An older woman with a severe bun and tired eyes met them. Tack showed his badge and asked to see the Sagets.

The housekeeper led them out back to a large covered patio with an outdoor kitchen and brick oven. Mr. and Mrs. Saget sat at the table together, sipping mimosas, as the guy from the pool place worked on opening up their pool for summer. Seemed a little late. It was swim weather now.

"Ranger Holliday," Mrs. Saget said and stood, her eyes trailing to Chelsey. Tack introduced her to Brick and Donna and explained why they'd come.

"You think whoever killed the housekeeper from Redd Rock also murdered Rosa?" Donna asked. Brick's nose was scrunched, as if the entire topic of conversation was garbage.

"It's possible," Tack said. "Which is why my colleague, Agent Banks, needs to ask a few questions, most of which you've already answered. Would that be okay?"

"Of course," Brick said and motioned for them to take seats at the rectangular wrought iron table, but Chelsey picked up on his tight expression and rigid posturing denoting Brick Saget as a controlling man, uncomfortable with the situation. Not necessarily an indicator he was a murderer, but it did lend to his personality and would aid in Chelsey's tactics and line of questioning.

He needed a false sense of control. "Thank you for letting me have a seat, Mr. Saget. I know we're interrupting your precious time." She sat at the far end of the table, near Donna, giving Saget the impression of submission. But he was far from in control of this situation.

Mr. Saget smiled, and it reached his eyes; his shoulders were raised and chest puffed, showing pleasure at his role of dominance as he exercised his power. Tack moved to sit beside Mr. Saget, but Chelsey caught his eye and redirected him to sit closer to her.

Chelsey glanced at Donna. Hands in her lap, rapid blinking. Head down. An easy mark. Or...feigning insecurity. If she'd been deceitful in her pregnancies, then she was calculating and crafty. But the killer was a man. Didn't mean she wasn't complicit or an accomplice.

Chelsey widened her eyes, a show of innocence, and leaned slightly forward as if gravitating and ready to hang on every word out of Brick Saget's mouth, then hunched slightly—another posture of submission, which he clearly enjoyed. "How long did Rosa work for you?"

Brick inhaled deeply, not in a hurry to be at her beck and call with answers. Typical display of authority and dominance. "Six months. She came in April and went missing in September. She picked up the children from school, then brought them home and prepared a snack, helped with homework and occupied them until about six. She did a little light housekeeping as well. In summer, she worked full-time taking the kids on field trips and watching them here."

"She ever take the kids down to the stables to ride horses? Swim in the pool with them?"

"Of course," he said. A man who needed control, but how would he respond to rejection? She shifted toward

Donna now and focused her sole attention on her face. Twofold. Test Mr. Saget and observe Donna when she asked the next question. It would speak to Donna Saget's knowledge or lack of concerning Mr. Saget's wandering eye and possibly hands.

"Any particular man take an interest in her, Donna?" she asked, calling her by her first name and thereby taking away Saget's authority. Not Mrs. Saget—an extension of him—but her as her own person.

For a split second, she glanced her husband's way. Couldn't help herself. Body language often was instinctive, unlike verbal communication. It was harder for the body to lie than the tongue. The tongue was its own entity. Like a rudder of a ship. Tiny but powerful. She hadn't learned that from Quantico training but the Bible.

"I don't know," she responded.

But she did know. Her body language had betrayed her. Mr. Saget had noticed Rosa. About six-one and physically fit. Hunting girls who worked for him wasn't smart, though. Unless he wanted it to appear that way. So stupid they overlooked it. That fit the profile—a killer who thought he was smarter than the law. Someone who felt a thrill taking risks and murdering women employees was a serious risk.

She needed those facial reconstructions to connect the former victims with nannies on Saget's ranch!

"Did Rosa ever talk about what she did for entertainment on her days off?"

Donna eyed Mr. Saget, and Chelsey leaned toward the table, blocking her view. This would keep Mr. Saget from having power, and it was one more step toward hopefully getting him to show some true colors. "I'm not sure what she did other than attend church at the Horizon Assembly in town. It's in the building that used to be Happy Hair."

Chelsey glanced at Tack to see if he'd acknowledge he already had that information. His brow had created a divot. Guess he didn't know that.

"What about the women you hired before Rosa? Ranger Holliday has a list of former employees. Can you tell me why there was such great turnover, and would you know where they ended up after leaving River Valley Bend?"

Donna's eyes narrowed, and her mouth hardened. "Why does it matter?" Chelsey had struck a chord, and it did not sound melodious.

"Because we have several dead women. All within one burial site in Big Bend. Surely you saw that on the news a few months ago. Naturally, we're going to wonder if there's a connection to their deaths and Rosa's."

Brick slammed his glass onto the table with a clink, and his jaw ticked. Eyes narrowed. Tight fists. "You think we're murdering the help? Why, because they didn't do their jobs well?"

Yes, put the blame on the law enforcement. Redirect. Deflect. He was clearly hiding something. Might not be the murders. Could be his philandering ways. Could be both. "No one said you or your wife are murdering anyone. But you have a lot of men that work this ranch, and it's possible one of them might have. We aren't ruling anyone out, but we have a forensic anthropologist working to develop a time frame of when the victims died, which will help us secure alibis to officially rule you out. And she's doing facial reconstructions. Then we'll be back to see if you recognize them."

She waited a beat to see what his response would tell

her from the knowledge that these victims would have faces and voices from the grave. He sat like stone, staring her down, unblinking. A show of intimidation.

Donna shifted in her chair, revealing utter discomfort. From the palpable tension or the fact she or her husband might have something to do with the murders, Chelsey couldn't say.

"By the way, who is nannying your children now?" Chelsey asked.

"Her name is Patricia, but I don't know why that's important," Donna said in a clipped tone.

Patricia might be able to confirm if Brick was as handsy as the rumors portrayed. It could go to motive. "It's probably not. Is she here legally?" She held up her hands. "I'm not ICE. But we don't know if there's any record of these victims—even if we can create faces for them. This information would help us build a profile and aid the investigation."

Donna shot Brick another glance, but this was more annoyed than nervous. They had hired illegal immigrants, and she hadn't liked it. Brick Saget didn't abide by rules if he could benefit. His decisions were based on selfishness and perhaps financial greed. What other ethical rules did he ignore?

When Donna clearly refused to answer, Brick stood, towering their seated positions. "You can talk to us through our lawyers. We've been as helpful as we can."

Not can. As helpful as they wanted to be. "It's okay. Once we have those facial reconstructions, we'll be able to determine if they were here on a visa or not and connect them to places of employment." She smiled with a whole helping of saccharine. "Good day."

Tack resolutely nodded and followed Chelsey toward the truck. "You're quite pleasant," he said woodenly.

"He's guilty of something."

"Could just be of hiring illegal immigrants."

"Maybe. I imagine when we get some identification on the victims, we'll find one or more did in fact work for the Sagets at some point." She fanned herself with her hand. "When do the kids get out of school?"

"How would I know?"

She frowned. "I would have liked to have bumped into Patricia. Ask her about Brick."

"And get no answer. She rats out her boss, she loses her job and could be blacklisted at other ranches. But who knows. I can't say what her situation is."

Probably not stellar. The killer felt powerful targeting these women. Silencing them. Could he be someone who had no authority, or was he a man like Brick who did indeed wield power and it corrupted him, made him believe he could do and take what he wanted?

"You're working your profile. You need ice?"

No, she needed to stop second-guessing herself so much.

EIGHT

As they neared their vehicle, a white truck pulled around the drive and a muscular guy about six-one clambered out, his boots dirty and his shirt pristine and tight around his biceps.

"Anthony?" Chelsey called, a dumbfounded expression on her face.

The man did a double take and grinned as he approached. "Miss Chelsey—"

"Just Chelsey," she corrected.

The man—late thirties, Hispanic descent—grinned and nodded. "Right. What you up to?"

"I was going to ask you the same thing."

Tack waited impatiently for the introduction. Chelsey pointed to him then as if she cued in on his irritation. "This is Ranger Holliday. We're investigating a murder."

"Izzy's?" he asked and extended a weather-worn hand.

"This is Anthony Gonzalez. He's the property manager for Redd Rock Ranch."

That explained how he knew Izzy. Did not explain what he was doing at the Sagets'. Tack noticed the huge magnetic sign on the side of his truck—Lonestar Ranch

Management. "Are you the property manager for the Sagets?" Tack asked.

Chelsey pivoted to inspect his truck, then looked at Anthony.

"I am. About eight months. Though Mr. Saget has had me out to do work over the past few years. I think he's testing me." He grinned again.

"What exactly do you do?" Tack asked.

Anthony's smile faded as it dawned on him this was more than small talk. "Uh… I come out monthly and check the property. Fencing, roads, ponds, docks…it's thorough. A lot of ranchers hire out."

"We met the first day I was on Redd Rock," Chelsey offered. "Fencing issues."

He shot her a quick smile. "I have reports I need to get to Mr. Saget."

"Did you ever meet Rosa Velasquez? She worked as a nanny last year."

Anthony frowned and twisted his lips to the side. "If I did, I don't remember. I mostly work with Mr. Saget. I know he has a couple of kids, though. They're loud." He gave her a knowing look.

"Well, we won't keep you," Tack said. "Nice meeting you."

They got inside the truck and he cranked the ignition; hot air blasted from the vents then quickly cooled. "I wonder how many other ranches he manages. Gives him access."

Chelsey buckled up. "I don't like him for it."

"Based on what? The fact he looks like Mark Consuelos?"

"How do you know who Mark Consuelos is?"

Tack tossed her a wooden look. "Because you droned

on last time you were in town. During that dumb celebrity crush game you made me play at dinner one night."

"Oh." She smirked. "Well, that's not why. I can't believe you remembered that."

Chelsey had a voice a man wanted to listen to, and it was hard not to be engaged in her conversation. She made a dumb celebrity crush game fun and worth remembering. Although he didn't remember who he'd said.

"You still have a thing for Angie Harmon?"

Ah. The actress who played Rizzoli on *Rizzoli & Isles*. "Nah."

"Anthony isn't our guy. Doesn't fit the feeble profile we have established so far. I won't rule him out, though." She cocked her head. "But the idea of someone from a company that comes in contact with multiple ranches in these parts could be a possibility."

"Let's see if we can come up with who owned that silver pin from Big Bend Adventure Tour Guides. Izzy got it somehow. Maybe the owner of said pin will also recognize Rosa. If we can't find a suspect, we may be able to at least establish a link."

Chelsey slid her mouth sideways and made a clicking noise while pointing at him. "I like the way you think."

"Just the way I think? Really? That's all I got going for me?" he said with mock disappointment, but her remark earlier had rankled him. Why was Chelsey so adamant he needed a date, a relationship? Why did she think it was her place to be matchmaker? And why did it irritate him so much?

Six months ago a colleague at work had set him up on a date, and he'd had no qualms about it. In fact, Arlie had been a lovely woman. Funny. Easy to talk to. Her family owned an aftermath recovery and compassions services company and her job as a grief counselor, using therapy dogs, and crime scene cleaner was interesting. They'd gone on five or six dates and then Arlie had ended it.

He'd been slightly shocked, as their dates had always been good—or so he thought. She'd simply said, "Tack, I really like you. I think you're a great guy, but I don't see this going too far, and I'm looking for something that will."

She had placed a sweet kiss on his cheek and exited his truck and his life.

"Nah, that's not all you've got going for you. You've got good bone structure—not a ploy to bring up Charlotte again, by the way." Chelsey dug through her purse, retrieving a cinnamon breath mint. "Want one?"

"Sure. Let's add fresh breath to good brains and bones." He held out his palm, and Chelsey placed the mint in the middle, the tips of her fingers brushing along his skin and sending a zing into his abdomen. He ignored the sensation and popped the mint in his mouth. "Hey, do I give off the noncommittal vibe?" Surely that was what Arlie must have meant by saying she didn't see it going further. She was for it. Clearly, she didn't think he was. Why?

"Is this about Charlotte?" Chelsey asked and crunched into her mint. She was going to break a tooth someday. What was it about crunching that appealed to her so much?

"No," he drawled. "Can we drop Charlotte?"

"Sure. To answer your question, maybe. I mean, you have swagger and confidence and you're flirty, so women may get the feeling you're cocky and not serious about settling down. But it would only take a few dates or an hour talking to you to know that you're not a heartbreaker but a homemaker."

"Isn't that a feminine word?"

"Aaaaand now you're sexist."

He snorted. "I am not. I'm just saying—"

"I know what you're saying." Her warm brown eyes held mischief and humor. One of his favorite things about her. "I meant a person who would rather make a home with someone than break their heart."

"Okay. I'm a homemaker." He nodded once. "I like it."

"I wouldn't tell that to your bros back at your company," she said through a laugh. "They'll say you've gone soft and ask for a batch of homemade brownies."

"That's sexist."

They both laughed at their ridiculous banter. It was fun playing off Chelsey like this. Easy. This was another reason why she was his best female friend. But not all his friends who were women sent his pulse skittering. And that was a problem he needed to remedy, quick. It made no sense. No sense he wanted to explore.

"Why are you asking that, anyway?"

"Something someone on a date implied in her breakup with me. She was looking for permanent and didn't see that happening with me."

"One, her loss. Two, it might mean she didn't feel you were compatible enough for her for a long-term relationship, not that you couldn't commit."

"Oh. Well, now I feel rejected in a whole new way. Thanks."

Chelsey snickered and popped another mint. Guess it was a substitute for ice chips. "I'd never reject you. Take comfort in that."

He parallel parked in front of the Big Bend Adventure Tour Guides and cut the ignition. "You did reject me. So…that doesn't really make me feel any better."

She unbuckled and waved off the notion. "I never did."

"I kissed you."

"And we both agreed it was awkward. We're like siblings. That's not rejection." She opened the door and bounded out before he could interject. He'd known the woman long enough to know she was done with a subject. But why should it make her uncomfortable?

He followed her into the brick building in downtown Gran Valle. The cool air and smell of tropical islands hit him. This wasn't the beach; it was Texas. The place was small, and the walls were lined with large black-and-white photos of tour guides leading horseback trail rides, hikes, zip-lining and rafting excursions. The front desk was tidy but empty, and country pop played from speakers in the ceiling. A guy with cottony platinum blond hair hanging in tight curls met them with a canoe-size grin and entered the lobby.

"Hey, man," he said. "Can I help y'all?"

He wore a blue T-shirt with the company's logo and cargo shorts.

"We need some information," Tack said, and the guy scoped out his clothing, then his eyes grew wide.

"Yessir, Ranger, sir."

Tack caught Chelsey's near grin. Respecting Texas Rangers was a good thing. Many little Texan boys dreamed of growing up to be a Texas Ranger. Granted, they thought it was all Chuck Norris style, but still.

"How can I help you?" the kid asked.

Chelsey stepped forward, showing her FBI creds as if comparing who was bigger and badder. Tack refrained from chuckling. "I'm Special Agent Chelsey Banks. Do you know this woman? Her name is Izzy Garcia." She showed him a picture of Izzy.

The guy studied the photo and shook his head. "Nah, I don't think so. Doesn't mean she never booked with us, though. I can check."

"Thank you," Chelsey said. "I didn't catch your name."

"Tyler. Tyler Upchurch." He clacked away at the computer with more skill than Tack would have assumed by his all-adventure build and appearance. Looks were deceiving. "I don't see any Izzy Garcia. I tried both spellings." He looked up. "Is this lady in trouble or something? Because our people are legit. We would never hurt or take advantage of anyone."

"She's deceased. We're trying to find any information we can about her. Friends. Boyfriends. Anyone else here?" Tack asked.

"Yeah. We've got several tours today, so we're all on deck. Some are out in the field already, though."

"Anyone mention the loss of one of their tour guide pins? Like the one that's on your ball cap." Chelsey pointed to a navy blue ball cap with Tyler's name and the silver pin on it. Identical to the one found at Izzy's.

"Actually, yeah." He turned his head toward the back and called, "Hey, Wally! Found your missing pin!"

A brute of a man with a shiny head and dark eyes waltzed into the entryway. "Where'd you find it?"

"I didn't." Tyler pointed to Tack. Wally took one good look at Tack's Ranger attire with his white cowboy hat and boots, his silver star on his coat pocket, and his eyes widened, then he cursed and bolted toward the back.

Chelsey was already hopping the counter and giving

chase. Tack pointed at Tyler. "Nobody moves or leaves," he said while sprinting to the front door. He tossed his hat on the chair by the door and rounded the building to where the employees parked. Up ahead the man was running toward the desert terrain that surrounded the business.

Tack wasn't sure where it was going to lead, but he clearly wasn't going to head for his car. Tack changed direction, seeing Chelsey up ahead as she roared for Wally to freeze, not necessarily being nice about it. She could be tough in word and deed when necessary.

Dust kicked up underneath his boots as Wally broke hard right and raced toward the shops only separated by small side streets.

"Don't make me shoot!" Chelsey demanded from about twenty feet ahead. Tack, with his long stride, was already gaining. It wouldn't shock him to hear the sound of gunfire, but Wally wasn't as stupid as he looked. He probably knew an agent wouldn't fire in a public place. As Tack turned down the side street that ran between a souvenir shop and a historical museum, he spotted Chelsey darting inside the souvenir store. He followed.

Wally knocked over a metal stand holding postcards, and Chelsey hurdled it in time to reach Wally, but he pivoted and charged her unexpectedly, throwing her off balance and knocking the gun from her hand.

Tack aimed. "Freeze."

Wally had Chelsey's head in the crook of his meaty arm and a survival knife at her throat. "You drop your gun or I slit her throat." He looked at the young girl behind the counter, who was paralyzed with her mouth agape. "You, get out from behind that counter, slow-like, and lay facedown or you're next!"

"It's okay, honey," Tack said and coaxed her to obey. She tiptoed around the register and slowly fell prostrate, her hands trembling as she quietly sobbed into the indoor-outdoor carpet.

Tack's heart lurched into his throat, and he held up a hand, keeping his gun on Wally. "Whoa, buddy. Let's talk about this. Easy. Slow. Calm." It was like when Charles had been held at gunpoint by the convenience store robber.

"I said drop the gun, or I'm taking her with me and slicing her when I get where I'm going."

Chelsey's face was steady, but her hand trembled at her side.

The man was desperate. His plan had gaping holes, and he'd never make it a mile before the cops cut him off. But desperate men didn't think clearly or logically, and that made them unpredictable and dangerous.

He swallowed hard. Tack hadn't been able to save Charles.

What if he couldn't save Chelsey?

The tip of the blade pressed into Chelsey's tender flesh, sending a stinging sensation and a wave of fear through her bloodstream. Anyone who claimed agents felt no fear were liars. Wally was irrational, frenzied and therefore dangerous and reckless. She couldn't anticipate his next move.

A flash of panic in Tack's eyes told the same tale, but there was something else that had him slack-jawed and ashen. Some other fear.

Suddenly, his blue eyes cleared.

"We just want to talk about Izzy Garcia."

"I didn't kill her!" he yelled, his hot breath brushing her cheek. She winced as his grip tightened.

"I believe you," she said with a calmness she did not feel. "No one thinks you killed her, but we think you might know who did. And it's clear you know something sinister, or you wouldn't have run from us and taken me hostage now. Right?"

His grip loosened. This man needed calm and composure. A woman would be less likely to threaten him. She'd already noticed his protruding forearm veins and unusually large biceps. He juiced. Alpha male. Chip on his shoulder and impulsive. Men were nothing more than rivalry to him. Tack's stature alone would feel intimidating to him even if Tack's arms weren't the size of boulders.

Chelsey caught Tack's eye and spoke through hers to tell him to back off, to let her lead the way out of this. It was the best chance they had. He needed to trust her. His nod was almost invisible, but he didn't drop his weapon.

Chelsey continued, "Wally, I know you don't want to hurt me. Just like you didn't hurt Izzy. What happened to her? Do you know who killed her?"

"It wasn't me. I—I loved her."

"And the man called the Outlaw killed her." She needed to remind him who the real enemy was. "He tried to kill me, too."

His grip loosened a fraction more, and she breathed easier.

"We want to find him, but we have nothing but your work pin. How did you meet her? And why did you run?"

Tack kept his eyes on Wally and his gun still aimed at him with a steady hand. Not a single shake. That was Tack. Her constant. Her steady.

"I…"

"Put the knife down. Let me go. You're hurting me, Wally." Her heart thundered against her ribs. His slight release did nothing to soothe her. He could make a split-second decision any moment, act on impulse and haul her outside like a hostage or slit her throat and take his chances on an escape.

Tack's gun slowly raised, and it dawned he was preparing to take a head shot if it got out of control. It wasn't. Couldn't. "Wally. Help me help Izzy. Let's figure out who killed her."

The seconds stretched like eternity ticking by. Beads of sweat lined Tack's forehead, but his gaze was resolute. Chelsey's stomach knotted and roiled. Blood whooshed in her ears. The cashier was still crying into the carpet.

Wally slowly released the knife and dropped it. Chelsey kicked it away and grabbed his arm, twisting it behind him and retrieving the cuffs from her pocket, placing the silver bracelets around his wrists. Wally never protested. Tack called the local sheriff and helped the young employee to her feet. She was no more than nineteen or twenty and terrified. By the time he got her settled with a glass of water, Chelsey had found her gun and kept it on Wally, who was sitting with his back against the wall underneath the window facing the street.

"Hey, sweetie," she called toward the shaken-up cashier, "don't leave your purse where it's visible and accessible." She pointed to the bag behind the counter. "All it would take is one con man or woman to come in and purposely break or knock something over to distract you, then steal your purse. 'Kay?"

The cashier nodded and quickly snatched up her handbag.

Tack looked at the counter by the door Chelsey had run through earlier. "You would notice something like that while pursuing a suspect." He shook his head.

She shrugged. Dad had taught her young to look for just that sort of thing. She turned her attention back to Wally. "Help us and we'll put a good word in with the deputies. You did assault an officer. That isn't doing you any favors."

"I thought you were going to arrest me when you showed up."

"For Izzy's murder?" Chelsey had seen the Outlaw, and he wasn't nearly this big. Athletic and fit, but not bodybuilder physique. She would have known instantly he wasn't the killer.

"No. Izzy had a friend who was in real trouble in Mexico but not old enough for a work visa. She's only sixteen. Things are real bad for her. Trafficking is where it's heading. I know someone who could help her. I thought you were here for that."

"For helping someone enter the country illegally?" Chelsey needed clarification.

"Yes."

"Have you done this before? And before you lie, I'm not interested in immigration. Not for immigration's sake. But if you've used this guy before, he might be a person of interest to us in connection to Izzy and other victims."

His gaze traveled from Chelsey to Tack and back again. "I haven't ever done it before—helped someone. But this guy has. He does it a lot. He's a good dude. Helps people."

Oh, she was sure he did. A real hero. "So he did this for free, out of the goodness of his heart, to help people?"

Wally shook his head. "Well, no. He charges, and a lot, but it's a risk, you know?"

"How much?"

"Ten grand."

Tack whistled low. "How did Izzy get that kind of money?"

"She didn't. She was saving, and I helped her some. We were waiting until we had it so we could bring her here. To be safe."

Something wasn't clicking. If Izzy hadn't actually done anything illegal yet, then neither had Wally. Talking was one thing. Doing was another. Presently this guy hadn't done anything but talk to someone who would do something for a fee. Money hadn't changed hands. Why be afraid of him enough to run from the law?

Lights flashed out the window. Wally would shut down the minute deputies entered. It would prove things were getting real. Like bars and lost freedom. But why? "How did you help her get the money?"

Wally averted eye contact, and his shoulders slumped.

"That's why you ran. Now's the time to come clean. Deputies are in the parking lot. Ranger Holliday has a lot of clout."

"Lot of bullets, too," Tack muttered as he rested his hand on his now-holstered gun. Chelsey shot him a withering glare. No point agitating the guy when they were getting the goods.

"I've been breaking into cars while tourists are on hikes, trails and rivers. But Izzy didn't know that. She wouldn't have approved. We were close. Only a thousand dollars shy of helping the girl she knows back home."

Gran Valle deputies entered, and Tack spoke with them while Chelsey studied Wally. The cashier's manager had arrived, and they'd been cleaning up the mess Wally had made when he barreled into the store. Deputies confirmed that vehicles and a few RVs had been broken into recently. TVs lifted. Wally copped to that, too, and the authorities led him to the marked units out front.

News media vans pulled up, and Chelsey's knees turned to jelly. Once she'd loved standing in the limelight assuring the public that they'd catch the bad guy based on a solid profile. Now, she felt nothing but icy dread. She had no clue who was doing this, and her profile was shaky at best with all her second guesses and batting back and forth.

Chelsey couldn't afford to be wrong. And the extra fear was there, because what if the news about the past profile had leaked and they hit her with that in front of all the lights and mics? Then everyone would know her mistakes. She could destroy Tack's good reputation just by his association with her. They might not trust his judgment when he was partnering with a hack.

Why hadn't it leaked yet? Or maybe it had in Dallas and the local police were taking the heat for arresting the wrong guy. It might not have snowballed to the Bureau yet. But it would. And if it didn't, the real killer was going to make sure of it. Was that his endgame? Toying with her, keeping her anxious and afraid of what would happen to her career?

Tack put an arm around her shoulder. "Well, I haven't been that scared in a long time. Try not to give me an early heart attack again. 'Kay?"

She smiled, but it was as shaky as the rest of her. "You were going to shoot him right in the head, weren't you?"

"If I was sure he was going to hurt you first, you better believe it."

"What if you'd missed?" she asked, knowing he wouldn't have. Tack was a crack shot and had been since he was a boy hitting cans with his daddy's Smith & Wesson.

"Then we wouldn't be having this conversation and it wouldn't matter." His easygoing grin brought stability to her teetering nerves. "Vultures are circling," he said and pointed with his chin toward the window.

"You take lead. I don't have a profile anyway."

"Camera shy all of a sudden?"

She punched his arm and frowned. But yeah. Yeah, she was. No, she was more than shy. She was terrified.

The minute the door opened and they stepped out into the blazing heat, reporters were on them like flies on a horse—impossible to swat away.

"Was this the work of the Outlaw? Is Wally Reynolds the Outlaw?"

"Did he kill Izzy Garcia?"

"Is he your attacker?"

"What can you tell us?"

Tack straightened his shirt, and his jaw twitched. He wasn't a fan of the media, either. "As of now we do not believe he murdered Izzy Garcia and attacked Special Agent Banks. When we know more, you'll know more."

"Should women be afraid? What advice can you give?" a dark-haired reporter asked, and her question felt genuine. She had the same physical traits as Izzy, Rosa and even Chelsey.

"Take all the precautions you normally would," he repeated from last time. "Lock your vehicles, your homes. Don't be running or jogging alone." He gave more common sense tips, then ended the conversation, and they went back inside the store. They'd slip out the back and return to the tourist business for his truck.

Once the coast was clear, they hit the pavement in silence, working their way back. "I'm going to call Jerry Allen again," Tack said. "My guess is whoever is smuggling people in is doing it from the border at Big Bend. It's a proven fact that patrols aren't strong in some areas. He might know of particular spots. We can then figure out who might be assigned to that area of the park."

"Could even be someone in Border Patrol." She fanned her face and frowned at her filthy shoes. "This could be our connection. The smuggler might be taking money to bring them over, then targeting them later, knowing they're illegal. Except in the case of Izzy and Rosa. Everything keeps us at a standstill until we can identify all the victims."

Tack swiped the back of his neck. "I could seriously jump in a lake right now."

"No, thanks. Last time we were on the water, we were human targets."

"Can't stop living, though, Chels. You know this."

She muttered, and they reached his truck and climbed inside. Tack let it run a few minutes, then blasted the air-conditioning and called Jerry Allen.

"He can't meet up with us right now," he said after ending the call. "How about we go over to Horizon Assembly, where Rosa attended church, and see if we can glean any helpful information?"

"Then we can go to the ranch to clean up. I'm feeling sticky and gross."

"Lookin' it, too."

"Oh, hush." She squirmed in her seat. It bothered her more than it should, even though he was obviously joking. And that bothered her, too.

NINE

Two days had passed since Chelsey had been held at knifepoint by Wally Reynolds. He was sitting in jail for his theft charges. And Rosa's church, Horizon Assembly, had pointed them to a few people who knew her well. According to friends, she had no boyfriend, and no one recognized Wally Reynolds's photograph. It didn't appear Rosa had tried to smuggle someone into the country.

But she had confided in an older woman, Lorraine Betts, whom she often spent Sunday afternoons with, that she had been sexually harassed by Brick Saget. At first it was lingering around her when his wife wasn't home. Compliments that turned to suggestions and then outright propositions and unwanted advances. Lorraine had pressed her to tell the authorities, but she didn't want to rock the boat.

Rosa had needed the job and the Sagets paid well and in cash and she adored the children. This went on for about two months and then, according to Lorraine, Mrs. Saget caught her husband caressing Rosa's hair by the pool. Two days later the Sagets reported Rosa missing from work.

Tack suspected foul play on Brick Saget's part. He ticked all the Outlaw boxes so far. He wasn't sure what role his wife had played, if any.

He yawned as the smell of coffee reached his nose. Bless Chelsey for making a fresh pot. He stood and stretched his stiff muscles. He'd been hunched over the dining table at the Redd Rock weekend ranch for over an hour looking through files and photos of employees who had once nannied for the Sagets. They'd been through them like Chelsey went through ice chips. All immigrants. All here on temporary work visas. Most of them here alone.

They'd spent the last two days tracking down as many as they could who were still here. Most clammed up, but a couple had told the same story Rosa had confided to the woman she spent Sunday afternoons with.

Tack sighed and collapsed on the rickety ladder-back chair. Chelsey brought him a steaming cup of joe. "You're my hero," he said, noticing her bruises were barely visible but she still carried a red scab where the point of Wally's knife had nicked her. Seeing her in that state had messed him up. He would have taken the shot had she not handled the situation with such professionalism and calm.

He'd never had a shot to take when Charles's life was on the line. What if he hadn't had a shot the other day? What if Wally Reynolds had cut Chelsey's throat in front of his eyes? The thought curdled in his gut, and he couldn't bring himself to savor a sip of his wake-up juice.

"What's bothering you?" Chelsey asked and slid into the chair, sitting in a cross-legged position. Talk about uncomfortable. His big frame struggled with sitting upright. "You have the same look as the day Wally had me at knifepoint."

She was entirely too good at reading people. He'd never told Chelsey about his failure to keep Charles alive. And now that she had a scent, she'd keep sniffing. It was her way.

He shifted in his chair. "Since you revealed your big secret to me... I have one, too, and I'm only telling you because I can't make you promise to come clean and hold nothing back from me if I'm not willing to do the same."

She swallowed hard and averted his gaze. "Tack, if you don't want to tell me something, I won't make you."

Since when did Chelsey not want to know every single thing there was to know? "No, fair is fair." It wasn't easy, but Tack shared about his partner Charles and how he'd died when they were Houston patrolmen. "I saw you at knifepoint, and I was afraid I might not be able to save you, either." And the thought of being more than friends, then losing her...nope. Never gonna happen.

Chelsey's arms came around him, and she kissed the side of his cheek near his ear. "Sometimes people do things we can't stop, even if we want to stop them."

That might well be true, but it didn't stop the anguish or the grief. The sense of loss. "Now, I guess we're even on truth telling. Let's talk about the case." He didn't want to dwell on his personal loss any longer, but he felt better sharing what had happened with Chelsey and seeing that she didn't blame him or hold him responsible. And maybe she was right.

"Okay, case talk." She resumed her position in the chair. "Talk to me."

"What if we only have the list of nannies the Sagets want us to have? Just the ones we could verify from work visas. If they had other nannies who were here illegally, then we have no way to follow up."

"We'll know when we get the facial reconstructions if the victims in the park worked for them illegally. Someone will recognize them as employees and spill the beans. Charlotte said we should have something by morning at the latest. I just talked to her. She said our oldest victim has been dead about seven years."

"Is she the one Charlotte almost has finished?"

Chelsey nodded. "I haven't given her Izzy's or Rosa's photos. Don't want to compromise her process, but I think we're going to see strikingly similar features. Now, what else are you fretting about that I can put to bed?"

"The mass shooter who's been sending you presents and letters." Chelsey's team had tracked the mail back to a post office in Dallas. But cameras didn't cover the parking lot, where cars could drop off mail, and nothing inside had turned up on camera footage that might tip them off to his identity.

Chelsey had come to him for help in finding peace during a scary and emotional time, and he'd put her into the crosshairs of a second killer. All her bruises and abrasions were his fault. "I haven't a been a good friend," he blurted and stood.

Chelsey paused with her coffee mug at her lips, frowned and set the drink on the table, the soft clunk the only noise in the house. "What are you talking about?" Confusion came through in the line across her brow.

He massaged the back of his neck. "If I hadn't put you up here—"

"I asked for a place that was quiet and secluded."

"And you came to deal with your struggles. Deal with what happened, and I all but forced you into helping me with a case, which has continued to cause you distress—physical and emotional. You aren't ready to jump into building a profile. I knew this. Saw it. I ignored it." That made him selfish and a rotten friend. He strode to the living room.

He heard the scuff of chair legs across tile, then felt Chelsey's hands on his biceps. "You are the best friend I have ever had. I can always count on you for sage advice, a good laugh, a decent conversation. You're reliable and kind. And you're honest to a fault, even when you tell me you need help on a case. When you tell me my hair looks bad and I stink from river water." She laughed, and he dropped his head. Too much emotion held him back from facing her.

"You've been everything I needed in my unstable, topsy-turvy, complicated life. Solid and constant—"

"Stop," he whispered. Hearing who he was from her perspective was overwhelming his heart. It was unraveling faster than he could patch the holes she was creating with her words.

"Tack, you're like a fortress for me. A place I feel safe and guarded. A place I can be myself."

He turned, his throat clogging with emotion. He was none of those things. Charles's death proved that. He was weak. Chelsey hadn't seen him sobbing over his sister's or Charles's deaths when his dad had been strong and steady. Not a tear shed.

"Please stop, Chelsey." He was losing resolve with every word. "It's not true."

"It is true. You want to know why I pushed Charlotte on you? Because if you had a woman in your life, I'd have to take back seat, where I belong. You say you're not a good friend, but the truth is, I'm not the good friend."

He framed her face, searching her teary eyes, seeing guilt and fear and something else in them. "That's not true."

He didn't give her time to protest. His instincts, his heart, ruled and guided him to her full lips. He met them with softness and tenderness, unsure of her reaction, but if what he'd just seen in her eyes was any indication, he wouldn't be rejected.

Chelsey gasped lightly, hesitated, then kissed him back with more force, her arms reaching around his neck as he savored and explored his best friend in this kiss. Far from the time he'd kissed her as kids. They were no longer awkward teenagers. There was much more than chemistry driving his kiss, and it fueled him to hang on.

He never let his hands explore further than her sharp cheekbones, her soft jaw, keeping the kiss like a gentle whisper. He'd never kissed a woman like this before. Didn't think he could be this way with another woman. He was careful but consumed. Chelsey broke away first, her cheeks flushed, but agony radiated in her eyes.

"You can't tell me that felt like kissing your sibling," he whispered and brushed hair from her eyes.

"No," she murmured through the most tormented smile he'd ever seen. It was breaking his heart. "But we're—"

"Friends," he answered for her. He'd been stupid. Hadn't thought it through. Hadn't let his fear over loving and losing lead. Now what? Was she just his best friend with some chemistry between them?

No.

Friendship had developed into committed trust and

openness. They'd seen the good, bad and ugly in each other and never fled the friendship. They'd fought and even hung up on one another, but she was worth apologizing to when he was cranky and frustrated. And he'd been worth fighting for when she'd called right back and asked forgiveness for being stupid.

He was already committed and in too deep. The image of Wally's knife at her throat punched him with enough force he took a step backward.

"I don't want to lose our friendship," she said.

He didn't want to lose her. Period. "Me, neither."

A knock on the door broke the conversation, though it felt finished already. Would things be awkward now?

"I don't want this to be weird," she said.

"I was thinking the same thing," he said as he approached the front door. He peeked out the small pane. "Uh...it's your dad."

"Then expect awkward." Chelsey sighed, and Tack opened the door.

"Tackitt Holliday," Mr. Banks said with his usual flair and charisma. For a man in his early sixties, he barely had any lines except for around his mouth, but the man always smiled. Zest for life and all, he guessed. "You are a bear of a man. Anyone tell you that?"

"Well, not in those words exactly." He waved his hand to welcome him inside.

"I didn't know you'd be here but I should have. Wherever you are, Chelsey is, too. Always been that way. I suspect it always will."

What exactly did that mean? Tack was too afraid, especially after that kiss, to ask.

Mr. Banks spotted his daughter, and his eyes lit up. She shared his full lips and smile, but that was where the similarities ended. Hayworth Banks was average height and fit, with a runner's build. His teeth were white and straight, and his hair was the color of straw, his eyes as green as olives.

"Hey, honey! I talked to Aunt Jeanine, who told me you were in Texas. I was surprised, since you never mentioned it last we chatted. I'm in town for a few days. Thought we could catch up."

Chelsey fidgeted, something she rarely did. "I'm actually working a case. Pretty serious."

"Well, you gotta eat even when working cases, don't you? And I drove all the way here from Abilene."

Tack wasn't worried about the tension he and Chelsey might have created with the kiss. There was enough tension between her and her dad to more than make up for it. But why would Chelsey not want to see Hayworth? They'd always been close even though he traveled most of the time.

Was Chelsey keeping something else from him?

Chelsey had too much on her mind and heart between murders and what had transpired only minutes ago.

She had no time to process or come to grips with that heartbreakingly beautiful kiss. Not one of a stumbling teenage boy, but a man with control, restraint and more emotion than she could imagine to fuel it and keep it going. She'd never felt herself tear up in a kiss.

Until this one.

How could one roughneck cowboy kiss with that much sensitivity?

Instead of figuring out how to deal with it and the reasons why she refused to let it develop into a committed relationship surpassing friends, she now had to deal with one of those reasons. Dad reminded her of the secrets she still harbored. When Tack had come clean with her based on the assumption she had done so previously with him, it all but ate her alive.

His kiss had revealed complete honesty and trust.

But she still held the biggest secret and had for years. What was she going to do? It was unfair to keep it from Tack.

"I'm sorry. I should have told you." What else could she say? It was hard to turn Dad down, though she'd avoided his calls—and there had been three today. Probably to inform her that he was in the area. Found out she was, too.

Before she could utter another word, he had her in a big hug. The smells of expensive cologne and a hint of cigar smoke enveloped her. "I missed you, baby girl. Catch me up on all you've been doing for the Federal Bureau of Investigation." He could call it the FBI like normal people, but Hayworth Banks had never been normal. Never average. He was bright and brilliant and by his slightly wary eyes aware something had been transpiring between her and Tack or he wouldn't have commented about them being inseparable.

Except where Dad was wrong this time—and he never was. She wouldn't always be where Tack was. Tack would eventually fall in love, and she'd take the back seat like she deserved. Or she'd get the nerve to confide the truth and he'd hate her forever. Either way, losing Tack was inevitable.

"You've been injured." He looked at Tack. "You been taking care of her, right?"

"It's not Tack's responsibility to take care of me. I can

take care of myself. I learned from the best." She half smiled and gave Tack an apologetic look.

"Fine. I smell coffee." Dad headed for the kitchen. "I like this ranch. Who owns it?"

More like whom could he swindle?

She and Tack shared a glance, and he sighed. "I'm going to walk out to the stable. Check on the horses. Give y'all time to talk."

Tack was being polite and not fooling Chelsey. He needed time to process their kiss as much as she did. Dad entered the living room with a mug of coffee. "Don't leave on my account, son."

"No, no," Tack said. "Go on and visit. I know it's been a minute." He placed his white Stetson on his head, making him even taller and more imposing.

Tack left out the back door, and Chelsey looked at her father. "How about we go sit out on the swing? They have a pretty pool, though I've yet to swim in it."

"The owners have a main ranch?"

He'd caught the whiff of money. "Dad, these people have allowed me use of their empty ranch home for a few weeks. They have been kind and generous, and I'm not giving you any information."

"What? A dad can't ask questions?" He sat on the lawn swing. The cushions were thick and comfortable. The moon was a tiny thumbprint as clouds nearly consumed it, leaving the terrain quiet and shadowed. The pool pump hummed, and the fountain created a puddling sound on the water.

"Of course you can," she said as she sat beside him, joining his rhythm to keep the swing from jarring.

"Then what's been happening? You're in trouble. I could practically smell it when I walked in." His strong arm came around her, and she wanted to kick herself for the draw to lean against him. He was good to her, but he wasn't a good man. "How can I help?"

"You can't." She told him about the Outlaw but refrained from informing him about the mass shooter.

"Baby, that worries me. He sees you as a threat and a thrilling rival. Men like that…they don't stop until they're on top."

That's why he steered clear of those marks. He'd set his eyes on women and more vulnerable types of men. Like Tack's dad after Cora had vanished. "Dad? Do you ever feel bad for what you do?"

"What? Investing is a risky business, hon. When folks lose money, I lose money."

He never admitted to conning, but he couldn't deny the tricks he'd taught and enlisted her in as a child. Had he assumed she'd forgotten? He'd lied so long he was lying to himself. "We swindled people, and you know it."

"Oh, we may have twisted the truth a time or two when we were down on our resources. No harm, no foul."

"You took advantage of Tack's family. You conned them out of thousands of dollars."

"That venture went belly up. It was legit. Why do you keep bringing that up? Keep insinuating I'm a terrible man and father. I provided for you. Put you through good schools and made it where you had circles of influential friends. I know business drew me away often, but I had to make a living, and you love Aunt Jeanine and she loves you."

He was right. No arguing those points. But he'd hurt people.

"And everything you are is because of me." He

laughed. "I kinda like how you're a chip off the old block. You and me, we know people. It's how you catch bad guys."

And how he conned good ones.

"I'm going to pay them back." Somehow. "And I'm telling Tack."

"Tell him what? You don't know anything. You have no proof, and you'll wreck a relationship unless...that's your intention." He sighed and kissed her forehead. "Is that your intention?"

To wreck a friendship? No. "I don't like secrets." She didn't like living a lie. Didn't like lying to Tack about anything. But her father had forced her to live one her entire life.

Dad stood from the swing, and it bucked at his weight lifting. "I can tell you don't want me here. It hurts, Chelsey. I love you, and I've only wanted the best for you. And I guess my best just isn't good enough."

He felt no shame. No guilt, but he wanted her to feel it. She almost apologized but refrained. This was not her fault. Even if she felt like it was. It was hard to hurt Dad's feelings, but he'd hurt her. Exploited her. There had to be healthy boundaries in place, and she had been weak in building them. "I guess it's not."

His eyes dimmed, and his shoulders hunched. Was he truly upset or playing the game? He was a pro. "I'll see my way out. Take care of yourself, champ. You are a champion. Don't forget it."

She squeezed her eyes closed, and when she opened them, he was gone. Like wind. Poof. Laying her head back against the swing, she exhaled heavily and rubbed her temples as she pushed herself forward on the swing, lifting her feet and letting it rock on its own.

Should some secrets be kept if telling them meant it might hurt another person? Aunt Jeanine would have argued to never keep secrets. Secrets were footholds to the enemy—he'd use them to trap you. Hold them against you. She felt that. Underneath the secrets, she agonized over the shame. It kept a hold on her. Coming clean would free her of that hold.

But it might cost her the one thing she cherished most.

Her friendship with Tackitt.

"God," she whispered, "I don't know what to do." It had been a while since she spent time in prayer and even longer since she'd asked for any kind of guidance and direction. She'd been guiding herself.

That hadn't worked out to her advantage. Everything was so much bigger than her. Why on earth had she thought she could control it? Even now she was calculating ways to be free from her guilt without revealing the truth. But one didn't seem to come without the other.

"And the truth will set you free," she muttered. But would it? In this case, it might be the final thread that would break an almost two-decade-old friendship.

A noise startled her. She sat at attention, listening.

"Hey," Tack said, and she jumped.

"You scared me." She relaxed and eased back on the swing. "How are the horses?"

"Good." He chuckled and sat beside her. "How's your dad? I figured he'd still be here."

Her chest tightened—that horrible nervous feeling demanding she release the hold by revealing the truth. But she couldn't bring herself to do it. Fear led the charge. "He's a busy man," she said, knowing it was a vague and weak answer.

Tack only lifted his eyebrows. "Okay, then, moving on. I want to apologize for that kiss."

That amazing, intense, achingly wonderful kiss. "No need. I kissed you back. And I'm not sorry."

"You're not?"

"No. You've clearly had practice since you were seventeen," she teased, deflecting the somber moment, the truth. At least for now.

"I was thinking the same thing about you. Not too shabby of a lip locker," he said, clearly picking up on her cue to keep things casual. To go back to easy banter and jesting. "Ya tasted pretty good, too."

She snickered and was inwardly grateful to him for being what she needed when she needed it. "Ugh. Stop."

He laughed quietly, and then silence fell and the tension built. "I'm going to bed. We have a long day tomorrow."

Tack followed her inside and down the hall. He turned left to the guest room, and she entered the master bedroom. After getting ready for bed, she switched off the light and slid under the covers.

But sleep would not come tonight. And if it did, she feared killers wouldn't be the center of her unwanted dreams, but that kiss.

TEN

The sound of movement woke Tack from a decent sleep. He sat straight up in the guest bed, his covers in disarray. Grabbing his gun, he listened. Cicadas croaked against the backdrop of owls hooting and a coyote howling in the distance. The air-conditioning kicked on and hummed methodically.

Thud.

Jumping out of bed barefoot and in basketball shorts and a white T-shirt, he slipped out of the guest room only to meet Chelsey standing near the hall, gun in her hand.

"Guess I'm not hearing things after all," he whispered.

"Guess not." She motioned him to cover her as she slunk down the hall, sleepy-eyed, hair up on her head and in billowy pajama pants with a matching tank top.

As she entered the living room, Tack backed her up just as the front door slowly opened. Tack kept a steady aim.

The foyer light flipped on, and his old friend Dusty Reddington dropped his duffel bag at the entryway, hands in the air, keys dangling from one and his eyes narrowed, his brow knit. "Um…put the gun down, please."

Tack sighed and lowered his weapon. "What are you doing here?"

"My house. I could ask the same thing." His dark gaze swung to Chelsey. "How do, Chelsey? It's been a while." He surveyed her briefly. "Nice jammie-jams," he said through a chortle.

Tack glanced at Chelsey and noticed the puppies and coffee cups parading on her pj's. Her shirt read, All I Need Is Coffee and Dogs.

"What is going on?" Dusty removed his dark brown Stetson and set it on the table in the foyer, then entered the living room. "Seriously. What is going on?"

"You don't know?"

"Clearly not. Rodeo got rerouted to Gran Valle instead of Fort Worth. The arena got hit by a tornado two nights ago. Thought I'd bunk in my house, but…"

Tack explained that Dusty's parents had allowed Chelsey to stay since he was supposed to be on a rodeo tour and about the attacks, which was why they'd had guns on him when he entered.

Dusty whistled low. "Whoa. Well, I can stay up and Mom and Pop's place. No big deal. It'll only be for two days, then we're off to Oklahoma, barring no more acts of God."

"I can't let you do that. I can get a hotel," Chelsey said.

He held up a hand. "Really. It's not a big deal."

Chelsey smiled and nodded. "Thank you. You haven't changed much." She looked toward the kitchen. "You hungry? Getting in this late, you have time to eat?"

"I could stand a sandwich. But I know my way around the kitchen." He grinned and stretched.

"Least I can do. Mayo or mustard?"

"Both?"

She nodded and headed for the kitchen.

Dusty rubbed his lower back. His hair was a little gray at the temples. All those wild bulls giving him stress. "How long you gonna ride those bulls until you realize you're too old? Leave it to the young men," Tack advised.

"Bite your tongue, friend. I'm going out on a bull." He eased down on the couch. "I really could have made my own food."

"Ah, let her do it. She feels useful."

Dusty chuckled. "Hadn't seen her in a minute."

Referring to Chelsey. They'd met at barrel racing a few times. And Dusty had spent a couple of weeks in the summer with Tack. Chelsey was always present. "No, it's been a while for sure."

"How is she?"

"Strongest woman I know. Brave and resilient."

Dusty arched one of his dark eyebrows. "Sounds like you're writing vows, bruh."

"Whatever." He waved off the notion. "You know we've been friends for a million years."

He responded with a grunt.

"One turkey sandwich on white," Chelsey called, and Tack followed Dusty into the small eating area. Chelsey placed the plate in front of Dusty with a bag of nacho cheese chips and a glass of cold water.

Dusty thanked her and dug in.

"Charlotte just sent me the reconstruction of the first victim. I already sent it to the Immigration and Customs

Enforcement agency. If she was here on a visa, we'll have her information in a few hours."

Tack looked at the photo from Chelsey's phone. Charlotte had done an incredible job. Dark eyes. High cheekbones and a soft, rounded chin. "This could be Rosa Velasquez or Izzy Garcia. Age range and everything."

Dusty peered at screen as if he was a child sneaking into a private conversation. Then he frowned. "I know her."

Tack swung around. "You sure?"

"Yeah. Yeah, man. I mean, I knew her. Her name is Josephine. I don't know her last name. I was more interested in looking at her legs. Sorry." He winced. "Not that it's speaking ill of the dead or anything. That's a compliment."

"Where did you see her? How well did you know her?" Tack asked.

Dusty rubbed his chin. "It's been some years since I saw her, but she worked the local rodeo."

"Riding?" Chelsey asked.

"Nah, she was mucking stalls. I flirted with her a few times, but she didn't speak very good English, so her smiling and nodding had nothing to do with my bad jokes." He shrugged half-heartedly. "She gave me a bottle of water one time."

"How would she have gotten the job? It couldn't be full-time, right?"

Dusty shook his head. "She worked cleaning houses." He held up his hand. "I'm getting the gist of this questioning thing, Chelsey. I know this because while I was getting ready, I heard her speaking with a local ranch owner. Big rival with Pops. Name's Brick Saget."

Tack's gut clenched. Brick Saget. His name was like

dust that kept resurfacing on a coffee table in summer. He exchanged looks with Chelsey, her nose turned up. "We're well acquainted with Mr. Saget."

"After she left, Brick said he didn't mind her cleaning skills and then alluded to finding out what other skills she might bring to the table."

"It's been seven years. You sure this is her?" Chelsey showed him the reconstruction photo again.

Dusty scratched his head. "Not to be crass like Saget, but you don't forget a face like that. I talked to her a few times, so yes. I'm sure."

She would have been attractive. Like the other women. "Did you know much about Izzy—the woman who worked on your family's ranch?"

"Nah. I'm rarely here, and as far as I know, she never worked the rodeos." He finished off his sandwich with a swig of water. "You guys need anything else? I'm beat. I have to be up early in the morning, and the rodeo is tomorrow night. You should come if you have the time. When's the last time you raced, Chelsey? Seems I remember you being pretty good with the barrels."

"A good while. I loved the rodeos, though," she said on a sigh.

"I plan to win. You should come and root for me."

And Chelsey called Tack the flirt. "We'll have to see where we are on the investigation. What time?"

"Seven. They sell Pronto Pups and funnel cakes."

"Okay, but don't get bent out of shape if we don't show," Tack said.

"Actually, could we come early? Poke around," Chelsey asked. "Show Josephine's photo to some employees?"

It'd be good to see if anyone recognized Rosa and

Izzy, too. Maybe the local rodeo was a connection—if the other two victims had worked in some capacity at the arena.

Dusty shook his head. "You're always working an angle, aren't you?"

Chelsey's lips tightened, and she blinked a few times. "Doing my job." That comment had struck a nerve. Hmm.

"Yeah. I'll be there around four or five. Gates won't open until six, but workers will be around. Let security know you're with me."

"Or I can just flash my creds and get in on my own," Chelsey said, and Dusty sized her up.

"You're still scrappy, too." He rustled her hair. "See y'all tomorrow." He let himself out, and Tack followed him outside.

"Anything about Josephine you didn't want to share in front of Chelsey?" Like did he date her or hook up with her?

Dusty flashed a grin. "A man never kisses and tells."

Tack pressed through his exasperation. Dusty was never serious. Never grew up. Just a rowdy cowboy and probably always would be. He needed a good woman to tame him. "I'm being serious."

"No. She was kind and pretty to look at, and that was it. I can't speak for anyone else. Now, if you need anything, like someone to rope that Outlaw trying to kill you, let me know."

Dusty's joke didn't sit right. Tack was well aware the killer was elusive. It burned him raw that he'd been killing women and attempting to murder Chelsey and himself and yet Tack couldn't lasso him.

"Dude, I'm kidding. I mean if you need me, I'm here

for you. Like I always have been and always will be."
He smacked him hard on the back, his macho display
of affection reminding him of Dad's hugs. Tough. Hard.
Strong. He'd never call Dad—or Dusty—tender.

"Thanks, and thanks for not booting out Chelsey."

"No worries, dude."

He watched as Dusty jumped in his black Ford 250
and his taillights faded down the road, then he went
back inside.

Chelsey had made coffee, and her leg was propped up
on a kitchen chair as she sat at the table with her laptop
open. "We have some hope."

The case did.

He and Chelsey, as far as romantic involvement went,
had none.

"Y'all don't mind saddling up?" Jerry Allen secured
his tan baseball cap with "Big Bend National Park" written across the front. "The station is remote on purpose.
In case folks who pay little to no attention to the rules
get off the beaten path and get lost. And Border Patrol
uses the station to rest, eat some grub. You know."

Chelsey's legs ached, but she welcomed the ride, even
in the blazing sun. Horseback riding had always been
therapy and peace to her. She could use some right now.
Rosa Velasquez had been close with someone who smug-
gled people into the country. Wally Reynolds hadn't
coughed up the guy to save his skin, which meant the
human trafficker was probably more dangerous than the
charges Wally faced for theft and attempted murder of
a federal agent.

Tack glanced at her, sighed. "You look exhausted,
Chels. Are you sure you'd rather not email? It's easier."

"I want that initial response—to see their body movements. Too bad the Border Patrol checkpoints at the north and south border weren't more helpful." But this area was most likely their entry spot. Secluded. Right on the Rio Grande. Sharing a border with Mexico, this 118-mile stretch was the easiest way to get into the country illegally.

Tack nodded and turned to the chief of visitor and resource protection. "Jerry, you heard anything about human trafficking in these parts?"

"Sneaking into the park to smuggle drugs or come in without visas occasionally happens. We only have so much manpower. But as far as anyone employed by the park being involved? No."

"And you've never seen these women?" He showed him the photos of Josephine, who Dusty had identified, Izzy and Rosa.

"Again, no. Do you realize how many people I see a day? More than I want to." He chuckled and rolled his right shoulder. "I used to think arthritis was for old people."

Tack smiled, and they drove over to the stables and saddled horses. They had to have them back in three hours for a tourist horseback hiking expedition, and the horses needed rest in between their riding and the trail hike later. Jerry promised, and they rode out through the terrain. He led, and Tack rode his gorgeous beast beside Chelsey's.

She'd worn hiking pants, which were breathable and roomy, and an olive green tank top underneath a lightweight cotton button-down. She'd tied it around her waist and pulled her hair up on her head. The sun was merciless, and although there were pines surrounding them, it was hot.

Mexican jays twittered in the trees, and hummingbirds and orioles flittered in the agaves. Surrounded by the Chisos Mountains, the view was breathtaking. She almost forgot she'd been targeted by the Outlaw and had another killer who was good with guns taunting her for her mistakes. The thought had crossed her mind a few times about the shots inside the ranch that first night. If a mass shooter was good with guns, he'd use guns. The Outlaw liked to strangle—but when his hand was forced, guns were as reliable as any weapon to get the job done.

Jerry stopped ahead. "Whoa. Sorry," he said and checked his phone, then growled. "I gotta go. Can you get yourselves to and from?"

Guess he'd gotten a text.

Tack tossed him a thumbs-up sign. "I'm pretty good with directions."

"Debatable," Chelsey murmured but grinned.

"Two miles southwest. Can't miss it. Sorry." Jerry handed Tack his compass and coordinates. "Cell service is spotty at best. Connor knows you're coming, so if you don't show in about twenty to thirty minutes, he'll call out a search party."

"I think we can manage." Tack adjusted his white Stetson and gave his horse, Heffie, a little kick and kissed the air twice. Chelsey followed, and they headed in the direction Jerry had given them. "We never really talked about it," he said quietly, "but things go okay with your dad? I noticed some tension that I hadn't ever before. 'Course, I haven't seen your daddy in several years. I get the impression he feels bad about that investment deal that went south with my folks."

The deal that was no deal.

"I don't hold anything against him. Neither do Mama and Dad. He knows that, right?"

She felt his gaze on her, and she forced herself to peer over at him. "They lost a lot of money. Are you saying they didn't take a crushing blow?"

Tack's lips took a downward turn. "No," he said. "They lost their savings and some college money, but Dad knew the risk when he invested."

Her father had hidden his sneaky ways even from his own sister. Aunt Jeanine, like everyone else, thought he hung the moon. A businessman who traveled the world. Pshaw.

"Is that what the tension was about? Him being at the house when I was there?"

"Sort of." She owed him the truth about her dad, what he'd done—continued to do—and her part in it. Actively at a young age and then turning a blind eye in adulthood. She'd worked hard to redeem herself with every killer she put behind bars, as if that one good deed would cancel out one rotten one.

But it didn't, and it never gave her an ounce of peace.

Maybe Dad had been honest and hadn't taken money from a grieving family that she loved. But he probably had. And he was right about it having the potential to wreck her friendship with Tack.

Was it her intention to purposely sabotage their friendship? No. At least, she didn't think so.

Tack's phone dinged, and he plucked it from his pocket. "I got the list of employees at Lonestar Ranch Management, and a list of ranches in a two-hundred-mile radius." He slowed his horse and stopped completely. Chelsey rode up beside him and hovered, but it was hard to read his phone screen in the blinding sun.

"Redd Rock Ranch and River Valley Bend both employed Rosa and Josephine—thanks to Dusty for supplying that information. I wonder who else employed them." He scrolled through the reports. "It's hard to see this on my phone. I need to print it out."

"I hope we can find an employee that we can connect to the ranches while the victims worked there. Before you say it, I don't think it's Anthony Gonzalez."

"But we're not ruling him out."

"No." She'd dug into him, since he'd been at the Sagets' ranch. Born and raised in Texas, his father and grandfather had worked ranches. He was the first in his family to go to college. He had an MBA from Baylor and was squeaky-clean. Never had so much as a parking ticket. According to his very little social media, he enjoyed rock climbing, horseback riding and canoeing. She wouldn't exactly call that dangerous living. His dog was a chihuahua, who often accompanied him to work. Not exactly menacing. "No, we won't rule him out yet." She'd proven she could be wrong about a person, with fatal results.

"Didn't you say Charlotte might have the next victim's reconstruction done after lunch?"

"Yes. She's going to send it to me ASAP. I'll forward it to my friend with ICE."

"A male friend?"

Chelsey rolled her eyes, but her sunglasses shaded it. "Yes."

"Anybody I know?"

"Doubtful."

They rode quietly. Hairs on the back of her neck rose,

and she surveyed their landscape. She couldn't see any-one, but it felt as if someone was lurking. She laid a hand on her gun and tightened her other hand on the reins.

They rode at a steady pace, and she finally relaxed.

Gunfire cracked, and dust near her horse's hooves plumed. The horse bucked, and Chelsey had only sec-onds to hang on for dear life as it whinnied and bolted.

Another round fired, scaring the mare, veering it off course and flying toward the pines.

A piece of bark above her head splintered, and she crouched, steadily working to regain control of the horse. "Whoa. Easy, girl. Easy." But nothing was easy. The horse was spooked and so was Chelsey, but she couldn't lose her senses.

She finally got the horse calmer when another shot rang out and the mare bucked again. She lost her grip and it threw her over its head. She went airborne, thrashing and grasping for anything to break her fall.

She landed with a sickening thud on the dirt-packed ground, and her breath left her lungs.

Tack jumped off his horse and knelt beside her. "Talk to me."

Chelsey shook her head, unable to expel a breath or sound. After a few seconds, she inhaled deeply. "I'm… I'm okay." Her head throbbed, and her tailbone might be bruised. "But—" Her words died on her lips as Tack's eyes widened and he leaped backward.

"Chels. Don't. Move."

"Why?" Dread pooled in her gut, leaving her light-headed. Instinct said dart away from unseen danger, but wisdom and Tack's face said freeze.

"There's a Western diamondback right…beside… your hand."

ELEVEN

Tack's gut twisted as he calculated the scenarios. If Chelsey so much as moved, the snake would strike and the venom would kill her within minutes.

And he'd lose her forever.

However, her hand was less than an inch from the coiled serpent, and he risked shooting off a digit if he popped the snake with his gun.

Chelsey's brow beaded with sweat, and it slithered down her grimy cheeks, creating muddy paths to her neck, but she remained statue-still, her breathing calm and even and her eyes locked on his. "What are you going to do?" she whispered without moving her lips.

"Well, I was thinking about shootin' it."

The shooter—whoever he was—might not be able to get a good aim without revealing himself, and he clearly wanted to remain hidden. Tack's gunfire might clue him in and draw him out. But time was ticking.

"Are you being serious?" she asked, but it sounded more like a squeak. She slowly cut her eyes and whimpered as the snake's triangular head raised and its tongue flitted in the air. The white and black bands above his rattler stayed quiet. Good. Quiet was good. The minute it startled rattling, it was over.

"If you move, Chels…"

She brought her gaze back to his. Big brown eyes bored into his with a mixture of fear, hope and trust. "Okay. Do it. I believe in you."

Her faith in him swelled in his chest. He whispered a prayer for God to guide his aim and glanced at Chelsey once more. Her resolute expression gave him the courage he needed.

"On three." She whispered one, and he pulled the trigger. The deadly snake blew backward, unmoving, and Chelsey rubbed her ear from the ringing of the gunfire. "I said on three."

"I'm not sure we had three seconds."

Chelsey hobbled up and rubbed her hand. "I felt the heat." She arched her back and sighed, then scrambled to eat up the distance between them. "I owe you one."

He tucked a hair stuck to her cheek behind her ear. "Let's see if we can get your horse rounded up." Tack had had the good sense to keep a hold of his horse's reins with his free hand.

After a few whistles, it was pointless. "We're closer to Jerry's office than the ranger station. I think it wiser to go back. I have no idea if the shooter is out there or not. Hopefully, my gunfire has him thinking twice if he is in wait."

She nodded. "So much for the downtime to relieve some stress by horseback riding. We should have just emailed the photos."

"Yeah, but you like to study body language. Can't hide a first reaction." He whistled through his fingers one last time, but no go.

"True. And by the way, I find it interesting that Jerry got a text and as soon as he bolted the gunfire erupted."

"Jerry's a solid guy. I will admit he's an adrenaline junkie but…"

"But that fits the profile."

"You can look into him, Chels," he said as he motioned her to climb up in his horse's saddle, "but he's not the Outlaw." Tack kept his alert attention on their surroundings. She grunted as she swung her leg over. "Anything need medical attention?"

When the mare had thrown her, everything went slow-mo for Tack. He'd watched helplessly as the horse tossed her like a rag doll and he'd had to endure her body hitting the hard-packed earth with a sickly thud. He'd been terrified by the horror.

"No. I need a new bottle of pain reliever, though. And I will have Duke and Vera look into him." Once she positioned herself in the saddle, he gave her the reins and swung up behind her, riding the bare end of the horse. His arms went around her as he regained the reins, her flowery-scented hair grazing his cheek.

"Fine. Ready?" he asked with more emotion in his throat than he wished to reveal.

"Yep," she murmured, and he wondered if their nearness affected her, too. He guided the horse in the opposite direction, both of them holding their guns and breath as they awaited another unseen ambush. His adrenaline raced until they finally reached Jerry Allen's office.

Inside the desk was littered with stacks of paperwork, multiple empty mugs and a few hunting trophies, and a wall was lined with photos of Jerry's expeditions skydiving, swimming with sharks and bungee jumping. Dude was a thrill-seeker, but not the Outlaw.

His secretary said he'd had an emergency and never made it back to the office. Tack would call and warn him about the shooter once they got back in the truck and Chelsey would have a few questions of her own if she suspected him. Now that they had some Wi-Fi, Tack emailed the photos of Josephine, Rosa and Izzy to the rangers for a hopeful identification. But he wasn't going to hold his breath. Jerry's secretary notified the rangers of Chelsey's horse out there roaming, and they promised to find her.

After going through a greasy burger joint and buying cheeseburgers, shakes and onion rings, Tack drove back to the ranch, where they could clean up, work from laptops and rest awhile. Chelsey immediately swallowed two pain relievers and headed for the master bedroom. A few minutes later, he heard the shower.

He texted Dusty to tell him they might or might not make it to the rodeo due to guns and rattlesnakes. To which he got a response saying not to come, he didn't need them bringing their misfortune with them. Tack chuckled and decided to clean up, too. By the time he entered the kitchen, Chelsey had already made a pot of coffee for Tack and was sitting at the table with her own cup of ice. Time to get down to work, then.

She'd left her hair to air dry, and it hung below her shoulders. He'd left his hair wet, too, and it was already a curling disaster without any product to tame it.

He quietly poured himself a cup and sat across from Chelsey. "How you feeling?"

"Like I got thrown from a horse after being shot at then nearly killed by a snake and almost had my hand blown off. I feel on top of the world." She narrowed her eyes and shook several pieces of ice into her mouth. The first crunch was the loudest.

Okay, then.

"Got the second victim's reconstruction and information," she said with zero sarcasm. "Midtwenties. Been dead about five years." She showed him the photo reconstruction from her phone. The woman resembled the others. "I sent it to my ICE contact to run through their database and see if he can match it with a visa photo."

"Good."

They spent the next couple of hours working from their laptops, making calls and sending out the photos. Tack opened up the list he'd received from Lonestar Ranch Management as a truck pulled up. "I wonder if his ears were burning."

"Who?" Chelsey peered up and out the front windows.

Anthony Gonzalez got out of the truck, and Chelsey opened the front door before he knocked.

"Hey, Anthony. How can we help you?" she asked.

Tack sidled up beside her, sizing up Gonzalez. He acknowledged Tack with a chin dip. "I wanted to let you know I'd be on the property for a couple of hours. Inspection. With everything going on, I didn't want to surprise you by being here."

"Thanks for the heads-up. Do what you need. We won't be here but about another hour or so anyway. Rodeo is calling us."

"Enjoy it. Looks like maybe you could use some time off." He motioned to her fading bruises and a few new ones.

"No rest for the weary or something like that," Chelsey said and grinned. "Oh, wait." She hurried back inside and grabbed her phone, then returned to the front door. "Do you recognize either of these women?"

Anthony looked at the photo of Josephine, the Outlaw's probable first victim from seven years ago, and shook his head. "No, I'm sorry. I don't recognize her."

"What about her?" Chelsey swiped to the latest reconstructed victim from five years ago. Gonzalez studied it. "She looks a little like Maria Dominguez. I can't say for sure, though."

"Who's Maria?"

"She worked for the Sagets at River Valley Bend as a nanny, and she worked as a rodeo clown at the local arena." He pointed to his shoulder. "I used to ride. Loved it, but a bull gored my shoulder and that was that. Doc said no more." He rolled his left shoulder. "Still gives me fits, especially the past few days. Maybe rain is coming."

"I'm sorry to hear that," Chelsey said. "Do you know if Maria was here on a visa or…?" She let her words hang.

"I don't know those kinds of details. Sorry. I gotta get to the property now." His smile was tight, and he turned and headed toward the stable.

"You believe him?"

"I don't know." Her phone rang, and she answered. He couldn't hear words, but a man's voice was on the other end, and he didn't sound happy. Chelsey closed her eyes and leaned her head against the wall.

Tack whispered, "What's going on?"

She held up a finger. "I see. Well, it was only a matter of time. Do you know where the leak came from?" She swallowed and nodded as if the man on the other end could see it. "I will. Okay." She ended the call with a weak press of a button. "The Dallas PD doesn't want all the backlash from Marty Stockton's wrongful arrest and conviction, so I just got thrown under the bus." Rushing back to her laptop, she clacked on the keys until the local news in Dallas came to life.

A large man with a bushy mustache and hooded dark eyes spoke to the press. "We are terribly sorry an innocent man went to prison for a crime he didn't commit, and we all feel the sorrow of knowing he was murdered inside that prison. However, our officers did their jobs thoroughly and worked the facts based on the profile we were given by one of the top behavioral analysts at Quantico, Special Agent Chelsey Banks. Marty Stockton fit that profile, and while he was innocent of the mass shooting, he was not innocent of harassing and stalking women. We found videos he'd taken of women at home in their privacy. We believe he was a predator. I'm not making excuses, but I am backing up our investigative work on this case."

Chelsey closed the laptop and rested her head in her hands.

Tack laid a hand on her upper back. "You aren't to blame."

She raised her head and met his eyes. "Except I am."

Nausea racked Chelsey's body like she was on a dizzying theme park ride. She'd become the scapegoat, and she accepted the blame. As if on cue, she received a text from her colleague Duke Jericho.

We're combing over all the old case files, videos and interviews. Hang in there. Your profile was solid.

She replied with a weak thanks. If her profile was solid, Marty Stockton wouldn't be dead.

"What did your section chief say? I'm assuming that was him on the phone just now."

She let out a shaky breath. "He's standing by me, but we'll probably end up with a lawsuit. The family will sue the DPD as well for wrongful arrest and us for giving them false information. It's not going to stick. A profile doesn't hold up in court—it's opinion—but the media attention and my reputation…well, that's going to take a hit for sure."

She could kiss the talks about a book on her professional profiling goodbye. She no longer had a one hundred percent success rate to promote. "I shouldn't be working this case with you. I'm going to tarnish your professional reputation." And being more than friends would tarnish his personal one. No one would want anything to do with the man who loved and possibly married a woman who'd gotten an innocent man killed and who had a con artist for a father-in-law. "I may have to resign."

She wasn't blowing things out of proportion. Agents resigned for less. If no one would have faith in her work, then why do the work?

"Chelsey, everyone makes mistakes, and I'm not so sure you made one in the sense of working a profile based on what you had." Tack took her hand. "You've always been an overachiever and too hard on yourself. You aren't perfect."

"When it comes to this, I am." She wasn't trying to inflate her ego or ask for a pat on the back. It was fact. Her track record had been one hundred percent. "I'm nothing if not this job. It's all I have." All she had to redeem herself and to give back to so many her father had taken from—how many she'd helped take from.

She trudged down the hall to wallow in her shame. No need for Tack to see it. And there wasn't anything he could say to make it better, but she appreciated his attempt to console her.

Thirty minutes later, Tack knocked on her door. "What do you want to do about the rodeo? You want me to go and canvass alone?"

"Lord," she whispered. "I don't know how to fix anything. Or even where I went wrong." That was the end of her prayer. She had no idea what to even say. Guess her communication skills were rusty. Nothing in her life was as it should be, and she had no clue how to get a single area back on track.

"Chels?"

"No, I'll go. Sitting here isn't going to do any good." She glanced at the Bible she always traveled with but never read, which was sitting on the nightstand. Maybe that would be a good place to pick up the pieces. Instead, she left it. She had a killer to catch.

The rodeo arena parking lot was sparsely filled at the moment. But in an hour or two, it would be packed with patrons excited to watch cowboys try to hang on to a wild, bucking bull for eight seconds. The job was dangerous but could pay quite a bit for someone who was skilled. Clowns, concessions and all-around good fun were to be had at the rodeo. Chelsey had never dreamed she'd be here investigating serial murders.

Inside it smelled of hay, manure and the greasy foods one would find at a carnival. Oddly enough, the mingling scents didn't put a damper on her appetite. "I'm having a funnel cake tonight. That's all I'm saying." It was a deep-fried-dough kind of day, and she deserved all the powdered sugar.

"Yeah, you are," he said as he led the way toward the main level where the stalls contained agitated bulls as well as horses for racing competitions. Cowboys in heavy leather chaps swaggered down halls, employees wove through them with radios on their belts—clearly on a mission—and a few rodeo clowns in costume but no makeup rushed into the men's bathroom to finish prepping for the night's event. Excitement and antici- pation sizzled in the air.

Dusty rounded the corner in his jeans, black chaps and Western shirt with a cool swirly design on the pockets.

She grinned. "You the Timberlake of the rodeo?"

He smoothed his pockets and tossed her a wicked grin. "Hey, I can't just *be* good, I gotta *look* good doin' it." Dusty had always turned heads. Lean and full of sharp angles and flirtatious eyes. But he was no Tack. Never showed much of a tender side—at least not that she'd been privy to.

He cocked his head and her face heated as she real- ized she'd been studying him. "You profiling me?" he teased. "Or just admiring?"

Tack bristled.

"I'm doing neither." People always fascinated her, and Dusty was an interesting person. There was noth- ing romantic about it. Leave it to his arrogance to as- sume attraction.

He glanced at Tack and sobered. "Your tickets are in will call. My name's on them. I ride fourth."

"What's next if you win this one?" Chelsey asked.

She'd noticed several cups and trophies in the guest bedroom Tack had been sleeping in. Dusty had won several big championships.

"I move on to nationals—" his cocky grin widened "—where I could receive the highest award given to men like me who've spent a lifetime achieving."

"What if you lose?" she asked. Who knows, she might have won some kind of honor had she not made this latest blunder.

He leaned in as if he was about to divulge a big secret. "I don't lose," he whispered.

She related so much until recently. "I hope you do win, Dusty. Losing stinks."

He shrugged flippantly. "I'll never know."

She'd had an attitude like that once and was reeling from it. A defeating blow. She hoped he never had to experience it. He would take it about as well as she was—like swallowing shards of glass dipped in bleach.

Tack snorted. "I think all this head swelling is going to cause a disgusting explosion."

"Nothing wrong with knowing you're good at what you do," Dusty countered.

"No. There's not. But if it's not kept in check it leads to pride, and I'm pretty sure it states somewhere that pride goes before a fall."

He was quoting the Bible and knew it. Had her pride led to this demise? Had she relied so much on her own ability that she didn't believe she was prone to human error? And by believing that, had she ignored something, skipped something because she was so sure she was on point?

The idea sank in her gut, and she lost her appetite even for a funnel cake.

Tack held out his phone. "You recognize this pretty face?"

Dusty studied the reconstruction of the woman they suspected might be named Maria—if Anthony Gonzalez was right. The Immigration and Customs Enforcement agent had emailed during the barrage of messages she'd received after the mess hit the fan with the media. They had no facial match and she wasn't in the system as being in the country on a visa, which meant she might have been one to slip in unannounced.

"I don't recall ever seeing her, and I would have noticed. Looks a lot like Josephine." He twisted his mouth to one side and shrugged. "Doesn't mean she never worked here or attended a rodeo, though. Sorry."

"No worries," Tack said. "We're going to ask around."

They left Dusty to his prerodeo rituals like all the other cowboys to canvass the photos to employees and other bull riders.

Hair spiked on her neck, as if unseen eyes were fastened upon her. An instinct. Gut feeling. She slowed her pace and nonchalantly scanned the dirty, tiled halls of the arena.

Nothing but her own paranoia and jitters.

Employees and cowboys recognized Maria, giving them a solid ID, and older employees or circuit riders remembered Josephine. This could have been where the Outlaw laid eyes on at least two of his victims. He could work the rodeos and as a ranch hand. Many of them did a side job for extra money, and the halls of an arena were perfect grounds to pick prey.

"We have more to go on. Victims worked here and on ranches, though it does widen the pool of contact. Did he scout them here or at their place of employment? It

makes a slight difference, but still gives us a more concentrated profile for the Outlaw."

"I'd say tonight was a success. How about some
R&R?" Tack asked. "I haven't enjoyed a rodeo in ages.
It's going to make me miss my own young bull-riding
days."

They meandered toward the dirt-packed arena where
thousands of patrons would watch as bull riders blasted
out of the gates with the hopes of hanging on to a wild
bull for eight seconds. It was highly suspenseful and an
adrenaline rush.

Chelsey stood at the half wall keeping her from the
inside of the arena. She inhaled the smell of musky animals and thought of her time spent barrel racing. She'd
loved the thrill of being on a horse, feeling its raw power
and majesty as she wove in and out of the barrels. "I miss
the old days sometimes, too."

Angry bulls pawed the stall doors and grunted to be
let out. She unlatched a half-door and stepped into the
empty arena.

"What are you doing?" Tack asked. "You jonesin' for
the feel of being back with crowds cheering you on?"

Maybe. No one was cheering her on now. Except
Tackitt. She looked back at him and held his gaze.

"What?"

Her heart constricted. As much as Dad had applauded
and encouraged her, Tack had been her most honest
champion without restraint. "Nothing," she murmured.

"Something," he countered as he closed the distance
between them.

She couldn't talk about her feelings for Tack, because
they were jumbled and she already had too many other
things that were pressing to deal with at the moment.

"When I go back to Quantico, I'll likely be benched from field consulting. It'll be like my days in the arena. Applause, excitement. Packed house. But empty now."

Tack laid a gentle hand on her shoulder. "It's one thing to love what you do. It's another to think it's all you can do and that you are your career. It's what you do, not who you are."

"Not for me. I do it better in the field than behind a desk." How could she continue to make up for all the bad things Dad did if she wasn't trusted to do it anymore? "I was taught how to study people my entire life. I don't know how to do anything else that matters."

"What do you mean by that?" he asked, following her as she meandered to the center of the ring where she stood and looked at all the empty stands.

She might as well come clean in this dirty arena. "My dad—"

The sound of hooves interrupted as fifteen hundred pounds of furious muscle charged toward them.

"Run!" Tack roared.

The bull had already lined them up as targets and tucked his head as he ate up the dirt, malice in his eyes and dust billowing behind him. Tack grabbed her hand and whispered a prayer as they bolted from the bull.

Chelsey's heart thundered in her chest and her ears clogged with nothing but the whooshing sound of blood pulsing. She refused to look back, but she was aware of the bull's ever-increasing presence, its snorts growing louder. "Split up!" Tack shouted. "Go left and jump the wall on the other side—don't try to backtrack to the arena wall door. I'll go right and lead him away."

"No way!"

"Chelsey," he insisted and broke his grip on her hand,

"do it!" He shoved her to the left and the bull headed her direction, but Tack paused and waved. "Hey…hey, big fella!" Catching his attention, he kept his arms flailing and sprinted toward the south side of the arena.

Chelsey stood stunned. Tack was playing with fire. Where were the cowboys? From ahead she heard Tack scream, "Run, Chelsey!"

She raced across the rest of the arena and scrambled to the half wall, heaving herself over it into the stands. Then she jumped up and was running across the arena toward the area where employees and cowboys awaited their rides to find help when a blood-curdling yelp hit her ears and paralyzed her feet in place. Tack was being thrust into the air like a tissue.

The world shifted and tilted.

She shrieked. And from her side eye, four cowboys in dirty jeans and chaps beelined for Tack, one carrying a huge red flag that he waved to catch the bull's attention. The beast lost interest in Tack, who was now lying limp in a crumpled heap on the ground.

By the time Chelsey jumped the wall and made it to Tack, Dusty was already at his side. "Call an ambulance!" Chelsey fumbled for her phone. "Where are the on-site paramedics?" Dusty demanded.

They burst on the scene with a stretcher and medical bags.

Chelsey hung up and slid to her knees.

Tack was unresponsive, bloodied and filthy.

"He has a pulse," Dusty said.

Thank God for that. But what was the severity of his injuries? Sirens screeched, signaling the ambulance was nearby. Had the bull gotten out by accident?

Those latches were locked until go time and secure

in between. There was no way. She glanced up just as a shadow of a man darted behind exit doors on the west side.

A man who looked an awful lot like the Reddingtons' ranch manager.

Anthony Gonzalez.

TWELVE

Tack awoke to the sound of hushed voices.

"You're basically saying a good ole boy purposely opened a stall and released a bull with the hopes to murder, or at the very least maim, you and Tackitt. That's horse hockey, Chelsey."

Dusty. He'd know that irritated Texan drawl anywhere.

"I'm not basically saying that, Dusty. I am full-on saying it. I'm fairly certain I spotted Anthony Gonzalez, who's a person of interest. A lot of interest."

"I don't even know what that means. Is he part of the rodeo?"

"No."

"Then take back what you said earlier about cowboys." His tone was hard. Chelsey must have seriously offended him. She had a way of doing that at times.

Tack's mouth felt like cotton, and his entire body ached. He opened his eyes and slowly raised a hand. "Enough," he said, but without the force to keep them from bickering.

"Make me," she dared him, like a four-year-old.

"Enough," he repeated, and they turned, Dusty

holding his hat in his hand and Chelsey with her arms crossed over her chest. "What happened?" One minute he was running, then he'd felt a powerful force and woke up here. At the hospital.

"You got knocked around by Red Dynamite. Concussion. Bruised ribs. You'll live, like all good cowboys." He tossed Chelsey a menacing glare.

"Well one cowboy isn't good. The Outlaw. And I'm sure he was there and this happened at his hand. You said it yourself, Dusty. Everyone was busy. No one saw a single person unlatch the stall and let that beast out. But someone did. Let go of the cowboy code for five seconds."

"Was it Anthony Gonzalez?" Tack asked and forced himself into an upright position, groaning at his ailments.

"Perhaps. I came in the ambulance with you instead of pursuing him."

"Why would you do that?" he asked, irritated. "If it was him, we could have questioned him."

"Because," Chelsey said as if that was a perfectly good reason. "Dusty just got here. He had to ride his bull first." Her disgust was tangible. So that's what all the fuss was about. Chelsey had ripped into him for not giving up his eight seconds and the path to a serious trophy like she'd given up pursuing a suspect.

"Show has to go on," Tack said. And she should have followed whoever she saw in the arena. No one lurked then slipped away at a critical moment like someone getting gored by a bull. Most people hoped to see that kind of action.

Dusty graced him with a satisfied grin. "I rode that old coot for you tonight. And I won. Going to nationals."

"Good job, buddy." They fist bumped, and Chelsey stormed out of the room.

"I liked her better when she wasn't so mouthy." Dusty settled his hat back on his head.

"Then you never liked her."

"Bingo." He winked. "I gotta go. You need anything?"

"Nah. I'm fine."

The doctor entered, and Dusty excused himself. "Mr. Holliday, you came close to having even more frightening injuries than your mild concussion, abrasions and bruising." He rattled off what Dusty must have overheard—or what Chelsey had forced the doctors to confide against the HIPAA law. She could be persuasive.

"I'm releasing you."

"Good, because I'd hate to have to decline your invite to stay. I have work to do." Tack slid from the bed in a stupid gown.

"I'd take it easy if possible."

Key word being *possible*. "I hear you loud and clear." *And am ignoring it.* The doc left, and he hurried and dressed, then met Chelsey in the hall. "I hear you've been defending my honor."

She gave him a withering glare.

"What?" Was she mad at him? Tack thought she was mad at Dusty. Maybe she was upset with the whole world. "What did I do?"

Her chin quivered, but she pursed her lips. "You almost died." She smacked his chest, and he winced. She spun on her heel and stalked down the hall, blowing past a nurse.

When Tack finally rounded the corner, she was leaning against the wall near the elevator with her hands covering her face. "Hey," he whispered. "Hey," he said again and approached cautiously—he was bruised enough. He hadn't meant to scare her—didn't realize he had. "I was trying to save you, Chels."

"I didn't ask to be saved." She kept her hands over her face.

"No, you didn't. But it's what I wanted for you. I knew what I was doing."

She dropped her hands to reveal teary eyes. "You didn't have to see your big self being thrown into the air like a rag doll. Didn't have to see your limp body hit the ground. Didn't have to watch as paramedics worked to make sure you were okay. I had to see that and I... I don't ever want to see it again."

Chelsey flew into his arms, and he inwardly winced but welcomed her against him. "I'm sorry," he whispered.

"I love you, you know."

"I know. I love you, too." He kissed the top of her head. *In* love was a whole other ball game. He was not in love with her. And even if his heart tried to protest it, his brain led the charge with all the logical reasons it wasn't worth the risk. "I didn't mean to scare you."

"I know," she said as her arms caressed his back in a loving manner. One he could get used to, if he let himself. He wouldn't. She pulled her head back and peered into his eyes, letting her fingers graze his stubbly cheek. Tack wasn't an idiot. He was hyperaware of that longing in her eyes. The one that silently permitted him to kiss her if he wanted to.

But she'd made it clear they were only friends. These mixed signals were messing with his head. He couldn't afford a fogged brain, not when his heart was already betraying him. If his heart and mind united and overruled his wishes, he was done for.

He brushed hair from her face, debating and warring within himself. As he gave up the fight and descended, she stiffened. "My dad stole from you," she blurted against his lips.

"What?" Now it was his turn to withdraw. She dropped her hand from his cheek and her other from his back, putting a foot of distance between them.

"I've been lying to you my whole life. I've wanted to come clean so many times." She shook her head, as if she couldn't believe she was confiding at this time, either. "You were honest with me the other night, assuming I'd revealed all my secrets. We promised and… and I broke it."

"What are you talking about?" Confusion clouded his faculties as he tried to make sense of what she was saying.

"My dad is nothing but a con artist, Tack. He taught me how to do it—that's what I meant by being taught my whole life to study people, but to him they're marks. I've even helped him—"

She was talking faster than his brain was tracking. Then reality hit him like a hurricane. His parents. Hayworth's big business investment deal. They'd lost tens of thousands of dollars, which had forced Mom to continue working and them to downsize their home. "Are you telling me that he rooked my parents? That deal to invest was never actually real?"

Chelsey closed her eyes and nodded. "That's what I'm saying."

"And you *knew* it?" Heat worked its way through

his belly clear to his head; red dotted his vision, and he balled his fists. "You let him—"

"I didn't know he was going to do it. I knew after the deal was done and the money gone."

"How could you? Lie to us, then look us in the eye. How could you tell me even once after the fact that you loved me? Do you have any idea what love is at all? What friendship means?"

Chelsey's spine straightened, but she remained silent. Good thing. She had no excuses. Hayworth Banks had preyed on them. "Why isn't he in prison? You're an agent of the law. Does that mean nothing to you, either? No. Just your precious reputation as the best. Do you even care Marty Stockton was stabbed in prison? Or are you more upset that your career took a hit?"

Still she remained silent, but her jaw twitched and moisture filled her eyes. Tack's instinct was to reach out and make it better. Make her better. But he fought his instinct and walked away, punching the elevator button with force.

"I'm sorry," she murmured, loud enough for him to hear.

He laughed. Hard. Forced. "Unbelievable. You're sorry. Well, so am I." He stepped into the elevator, unsure where he was going. He had no vehicle. Neither did she. Air. He needed air.

The elevator opened to the lobby, where Dusty sat in a chair with his hat resting on his lap. Tack startled. "What are you doing here?"

"It came to my attention you have no way home." He smirked, and Tack shook his head. "Where's your princess?"

"She is not my princess." Tack felt his muscles tighten. The stress was too much.

"Lovers' spat?"

Tack collapsed in a chair beside Dusty and unloaded. After a few minutes of silence, Dusty exhaled. "I never liked her. She got points because she was your friend and hot. She's still one of those things."

Was she still his friend? Could he get over this news? Maybe if she'd only recently discovered this information, it would be different. She couldn't control her father. But she'd known what he was and what he was doing. How many more unsuspecting victims had Hayworth Banks swindled? How many were Chelsey aware of?

What was he going to tell Dad? Should he tell him at all? It was almost twenty years ago. Mom was now retired. They were happy, and they'd only recently received closure for Cora when his other sister, Poppy, had solved the case this past Christmas season.

He needed space, but someone was trying to kill Chelsey, and he wasn't an unfeeling jerk. That's why it hurt so much. Like little shards of glass rubbing against his heart. Inside, he was a bloody mess. She'd helped her dad con. When? How long? Why?

The elevator doors opened, and Chelsey stepped off, froze when she spotted him and Dusty.

"Guess we gotta give her a ride," Dusty griped.

"Yeah. We can't leave her to the wolves."

"Wolf, you mean."

"No. I mean wolves. The Outlaw isn't the only threat to her right now. Long story," he said before Dusty could ask.

Tack slowly made his way across the lobby, his entire body aching. "Dusty's gonna give us a ride back to the rodeo."

She nodded once. "If you want me to recuse myself from consulting on the case—"

"I do. But you happen to be a target, so until this is over, we stick together. Might as well use that taught knowledge to help solve a case." He wanted to curl into a ball, but that would be weak. Everything his own daddy had taught him not to be.

"And when this is over?" she asked hesitantly, her bottom lip wedged underneath her top teeth.

His jaw ticked as he worked to hold it together. It was hard to imagine Chelsey not in his life. She was the first person he called for good news, for bad. He'd shared his dreams with her. His life. But she'd lied. Had been lying. She'd betrayed him and his family by hiding a secret after they'd promised not to hide anything.

Her careful previous words hit him. She'd never promised to share old secrets. She'd worded it delicately. On purpose. Deliberately. Anger rose in him again at her deception but was quickly flushed with brutal disappointment.

"I don't think we can fix this," he said through gritted teeth. "You let your criminal father keep doing what he's doing. You hid what he did to us. What else are you hiding?"

She didn't try to hold back her tears, which only made him feel even worse. "Nothing. I wanted to tell you for a long time. I was afraid of this very thing. Losing you. I'm sorry. I messed up. I'm—I'm doing a lot of that lately."

He looked away; it killed him to see her distressed, to see such a beautiful face and have it marred by betrayal.

Racket outside drew his attention. News media barreled inside, spotting Chelsey and rushing her like a mob.

"Agent Banks, is it true that your profile led the police to the wrong man in Dallas and Marty Stockton died for nothing?"

"How can you make this right with the family?"

"Are you here on leave? Have you been terminated from the Bureau?"

The vultures peppered her with questions. Her face blanched, and her mouth was agape. She looked to Tack. He'd been protecting her, shielding her from the media. But he couldn't shield her from this.

He slipped into the background, feeling as big as a mite as he abandoned her to fight alone.

Flashes. Microphones. Voices bleeding into one another as Chelsey stood alone, unprepared and at the lowest in her entire life. She blinked once, twice. Unable to speak, to put on her professional persona and step in, large and in charge. She'd washed her face earlier, but she was a disaster.

She panned the room as hungry lions waited eagerly to devour her. She was on camera, and what would air was her blank expression and utter shock. Not at the media. She'd expected this.

But Tack had all but told her they were over. Without him, she had no one. Without her career, she was no one.

Buzzing grew in her ears.

This was all her fault. Why had she blurted it out?

Fear.

"Agent Banks, what do you have to say to the families of the victims who didn't receive justice and to the family of Marty Stockton?"

Tack had sacrificed himself for her, and she'd watched that monstrous bull lift him off the ground. It had bounced him on its head at least twice, then he was thrown to the dirt like he was nothing.

He'd done it to rescue her. To save her. He'd allowed the bull to punish him, mar him. Trample him.

Her world had turned upside down in those brief seconds. Turned into a world without Tack, and it had terrified her more than making a mistake, more than being judged and criticized by colleagues and the media.

And that meant there was far more beyond the foundation of friendship they'd forged decades ago. Time had built upon that stable ground and cultivated a union based on trust, respect and hope.

When she'd looked into his eyes in that hallway, the words she'd said a thousand times tempted her to say them again, but with a truth she'd never realized before. One she had buried along with all her other secrets.

Her father had been right. She'd wanted to sabotage it. She didn't deserve anything, including friendship, with Tack.

"Agent Banks!"

The room tilted, and she felt herself sway.

The one good thing in her life was gone.

A firm hand gripped her arm and steadied her. The room spun.

"Agent Banks and I have been through a great ordeal in the past few days. We've been working tirelessly to apprehend the Outlaw and bring justice to these victims. Special Agent Banks has been integral to this investigation, and her expertise has lent us more information than we would have had if she had not been invited in to consult. That's enough for tonight. No comments."

Chelsey allowed Tack to lead her outside into the muggy air and to Dusty's huge truck. He opened the back door and helped her inside, then climbed into the passenger side.

"Why did you do that?" Chelsey asked.

"Because it's true and because... I don't know," he grumbled.

Dusty hopped in the truck and tossed his cowboy hat in the back seat beside Chelsey. She turned her nose up but said nothing and shoved his dirty riding clothes to the floorboard. She waited for Dusty to make some kind of ill-mannered comment. They'd gotten into a scuffle in the hospital room over the fact Dusty had chosen eight seconds of glory over eight seconds of being by his friend's side.

Dusty's only response was that Tack would understand. And then when Tack had woken, he *had* understood. Talk about irritating. But she wasn't actually mad at Dusty. She was angry with herself over her swelling feelings for Tack.

She owed Dusty an apology.

Well, he'd have to wait for it. She wasn't up to it at the moment. Besides, he likely wouldn't accept it. By the hardened expression on his face, he was well aware of the conversation she and Tack had exchanged at the hospital.

No one spoke until they reached the arena.

"Thanks for the ride," she said and clambered down from his flashy truck.

Tack stayed inside a few moments longer, then exited and waved to Dusty. He stormed to his truck and unlocked it with the fob. Chelsey got inside. The wall of tension between them was suffocating.

"Do you—" she asked.

"No. I don't want to talk about it. I want to go back to the ranch. I want to go to bed. And I want to wake up and realize it was a bad dream."

So did she.

But they both knew that wasn't going to happen.

Tack drove slowly along the gravel road that led to the ranch. His lights shone on the porch, and his grip tightened on the wheel. "You see that?"

Chelsey sighed as a stark white envelope stuck out from the storm door. "I see it." She got out, trudged up to the porch and examined the letter-size envelope. Just her name. Agent Chelsey Banks. No return address per usual, but this time there was no *to* address.

Her blood froze.

He'd hand delivered this one.

The night had crept by for Chelsey. Unable to sleep due to heavy things on her mind—like the fact that the real mass shooter was literally on her doorstep, the Outlaw had tried to gore them to death using a bull and Tack was only sticking by her because she was in danger.

And she might be out of a job.

They could ask her to resign if politics came into play. Or maybe she ought to resign anyway. But then what?

She glanced at the clock. It was almost 8:00 a.m. She needed to get up and get moving. They were heading to the Sagets' this morning with the new information they had about Josephine. Around ten last night, she'd heard back from ICE. Josephine Juarez was here on a temporary visa when she went missing. She was twenty-four and from Mexico. No other family in the States. But she had worked for the Sagets as a nanny before she was terminated and accepted employment about fifty miles west on another ranch as a housekeeper.

Nothing had popped on the girl Anthony said looked like Maria Dominguez, which only increased the probability that Maria had been here illegally, and the other unidentified victims—for now—might have been here illegally, too.

Today was going to be long and grueling, but Chelsey was up for the task. The sooner she caught this guy, the sooner she could focus all her energy on figuring out who had actually killed the women at the Warrior Women Gym. Duke and Vera had reviewed all the old interviews with possible suspects, but they'd alibied out and it was solid. They couldn't find anyone who fit the bill as well as Marty Stockton. Which meant he could have been framed by someone who had detailed information about his secret stalking and harassing of women, so they were looking into Marty's life running that angle. When they had anything new, they'd let her know.

Chelsey shuddered as she thought about the letter from last night.

You're nothing but a fraud.

Tack had bristled at those words, but it was the last line in the letter that had him raking his hand through his hair and gritting his teeth. And the last line that sent Chelsey's heart into her throat.

You deserve to die.

THIRTEEN

The crick in Tack's neck was unbearable, but not nearly as uncomfortable as sitting next to Chelsey as they drove back to the Saget ranch. Too many coincidences were leading to Brick Saget. Not quite enough for a warrant to search his property, but enough to lean on him a little harder.

Had he been too hard on Chelsey? It had taken bravery to admit what her father had done and what she'd been privy to. But it wasn't enough to assuage the hurt he felt over it. She'd looked like a lone rabbit with ravenous wolves descending on her last night at the hospital. The media didn't notice or didn't care that she appeared exhausted, frightened, stressed and unable to think clearly. They didn't care if her face had gone ashen and her body wobbled. They wanted their pound of flesh.

But Tack couldn't do it. Couldn't leave her there for the devouring when she was in no shape to handle herself. She'd been dreading that moment and knowing it would come. It didn't come when she was dressed for the part of a strong agent. She was vulnerable and had taken his blow right before they swarmed.

Could he get over it? He'd told her no.

Even after the long hours of ruminating on the situation last night, he wasn't sure he could fully trust her. And not trusting fully wasn't trusting at all. He'd prayed and been reminded of Jesus's answer to the disciples when asked how many times they were to forgive. In a nutshell, His answer was to always forgive. That was a process he'd have to work through.

Right now it was too raw. Too tender. Twice he'd picked up his cell phone to call his dad. Twice he'd almost stormed Chelsey's room for her dad's number to give him a piece of his mind. He'd done neither. Instead he'd wondered what would happen when the Outlaw was behind bars—if they could catch him—and what the mass shooter's endgame might be.

And when all that blew over, then what?

Chelsey would go back to Virginia. Healing would be easier when there was space between them.

"You hungry?" he asked softly. They hadn't eaten breakfast before leaving this morning around nine.

"No," she said and stared out the window.

This was so not them. They were never at a loss for words. Never withheld words from one another. "You contact your section chief?"

"Yeah. Last night. I told him the mass shooter was here. On my secluded doorstep. Never once noticed being followed. Told him about the local press."

"And?"

"And no one is happy with being cast in a negative light. The Bureau has had to fight off all sorts of corruption and mud-slinging in the past few years. The media will twist this and wring it out until they can get everything from it they want. Not sure what that is, but I doubt it plays to my benefit."

Tack rubbed his neck and then switched his blinker on to get onto the ramp. "You think they'll ask you to resign?"

She shrugged. "Probably should. I don't know if I can do it anymore. I haven't even worked up a profile of the Outlaw. Not officially."

True. She'd have had one by now and had the media working to her benefit. To the people's benefit. "Something will pop."

"Will it?"

He turned the radio down a little. He didn't care for this song. It was about unrequited love and loss. It wasn't working to *his* benefit. "I don't know."

They turned onto the winding road that led to River Valley Bend and then parked behind a silver Mercedes and knocked on the door. The same woman who'd let them in last time opened it, and they followed her to the sunroom, where Donna Saget perched with her laptop. She closed it when they entered.

"Agents. My husband isn't home."

This might work to their advantage. "That's okay. You can answer some questions for us," Tack said.

She paused and swung her gaze from Tack to Chelsey and back again. "Have a seat."

Chelsey showed her the picture of Josephine, the first victim from seven years ago. "We know from her file she was fired for incompatibility with the children. Can you tell us if she hurt one of them?"

Chelsey needed to appear on Donna's side, assuming the worst of Josephine, build camaraderie and rapport.

"No, of course not." Donna waved away the idea. "She would never have hurt the children." Her tone hardened a fraction, and Chelsey used it as her way in.

"But what about you? Would she hurt you?" She leaned forward, laying her hand on Donna's in a show of support among women. "I fell in love with a man who has no comparison and... I trusted him with everything and he destroyed it." None of her story was true, of course, but Tack's admission of unforgiveness were words of destruction. Her heart was a mangled mess.

Donna sighed and nodded in understanding. "Brick's several years older than I am. I suppose that's obvious. He's a charismatic man. A good man, really. But he has some weaknesses, and I knew that going into the relationship—I had been one of his prior weaknesses."

Chelsey studied Donna, who looked very much like the victims, only a bit older. She was midforties.

"Who chooses the staff?"

Donna ran her top teeth along her bottom lip. "Brick does the interviewing. But I have a say, he leaves the child-rearing up to me. I love them dearly, but they're a handful." She laughed quietly.

As if on cue, the sounds of pounding footsteps and shrieks were followed by a deep bellowing voice as a little boy bounded into the sunroom wearing a cowboy hat, no shirt, shorts and cowboy boots. Could have been Tack decades ago. "Mama, don't let Eddie get me!" He giggled then straightened up when he realized company was in the room, placing his hands behind his back.

A man shot into the room with a grin and hooted, "Gotcha!" then made the same face as the little boy. They shared the same features. Ebony hair and eyes. Bronzed skin and dimples. "I apologize. We didn't realize you had company."

"Sorry, Mama."

"It's okay, baby." She gave the man who must be

Eddie a knowing look, and he laid his hand on the boy's shoulder. "Come on, bud. Let's go raid the fridge for ice cream. It's quite clear you're playing hooky from school today." He nodded at Tack and Chelsey, letting his gaze linger just a moment longer on her. "Ma'am," he said.

She smiled. "Are you on the ranch often?"

"Me? No. Just when I'm here to manage the books." He extended his hand to her. "Eddie Rodriguez."

"My son. Eddie's an accountant." A mother's pride radiated from her eyes.

"Did you know this woman?" Chelsey showed him the photo of Josephine.

"Yeah. She worked here." Chelsey showed him Maria. "Yep. She worked here, too." His voice softened at her name. He'd been friends with her, maybe more, or simply liked her. "What's going on? Why aren't those real photos?"

"Agent Banks and Ranger Holliday are investigating the murders of these women. It's been on the news. The Outlaw murders," Donna said.

He frowned. "Oh."

Chelsey showed him Izzy's photograph. "What about her?"

He shook his head. "No. I don't recognize her. But sometimes I'm gone months without even visiting, so it's possible she came and went without my knowledge. My family doesn't keep nannies very long around here." He eyed his mother and arched an eyebrow. The son clearly was aware of his stepfather's indiscretions and disapproved. After thanking him for his time, Chelsey turned her attention back to Donna.

"I'm going to be direct. There's been allegations from

women that your husband was harassing them. Is that true?"

The color from Donna's face drained. "I wouldn't call it harassment, but he has been involved with some of the help. To save my marriage, I fired them. I didn't want to see them blacklisted from other ranches, so I simply listed incompatibility. But my husband is not the Outlaw. He isn't a murderer. If the women on our ranch have been targeted, it wasn't by him. We have dozens of men on this ranch. Look elsewhere. Is that direct enough?"

"Yeah, I'll say that's pretty direct." Tack stood, and Chelsey followed suit. "We'll see ourselves out."

They passed through the living room, getting another glimpse of the kitchen. Chelsey paused. "He reminds me of someone."

"I was waiting for that." He didn't much feel like friendly banter, but... "He looks like your celebrity crush. Mark Consuelos. And Anthony Gonzalez."

She snickered, but her eyes didn't light up. The fun in their ribbing wasn't there. "True. We can't rule him out. He has the same build as the Outlaw. He may not live on this ranch, but that means nothing. I'd like to take a closer look at him."

"I agree." As they got back into the truck, Tack's phone rang, and he frowned. "Gran Valle sheriff's station," he said and answered, putting the call on speakerphone. "Texas Ranger Tack Holliday."

"Hey, Tack. This is Detective Ridgeland. Wanted to let you know that Wally Reynolds entered a plea deal with the DA and coughed up the name of the man who's been trafficking people into the country from Big Bend."

"Name?"

"It's the chief of visitor and resource protection. A... Jerry Allen."

Tack's gut roiled. He'd been under their nose the entire time. Knew the lay of the land. Had access to the entire park. Would know the hidden spots. He'd left them after a text came, then they'd been shot at. There was probably no real text, just an excuse to leave them alone so he could ambush them. He was former military. In great shape.

And there were photos on his office wall of him doing all sorts of thrill-seeking, risk-taking adventures. Chelsey's suspicions may have been right.

"Do you have him in custody?" Tack asked.

"No. We rode out to Big Bend, but the lady in the office says he hasn't been in since yesterday."

He exchanged a glance with Chelsey. He knew they had Wally. It was a matter of time before he gave up Jerry's name, and he knew it. He might have skipped the country. He had the money and the means. But was he also the Outlaw? "Can you get me his physical address?"

"Yep. We're waiting on the warrant now. You can meet us there."

"We're on our way."

The sheriff rattled off the address, and Chelsey punched it into the navigation system in the truck. They jumped off the interstate and headed for Jerry's house.

"According to this, his house is secluded in the Davis Mountains."

They trekked up the mountain highway, traffic becoming lighter as they approached. If it wasn't for the solemnness of their scenic drive, Tack would have slowed and enjoyed the gorgeous mountains.

He glanced in the rearview. A large truck was approaching fast. Before he could utter a word, it slammed into the back of this vehicle.

Chelsey lurched forward. Confusion muddied her thoughts, but then it dawned someone was attempting to run them off the road.

Mountains flanked them, and below was a steep ravine. If they went over the guardrail, their chances of survival were slim. She fisted her hands, her nails cutting into her palms as she prayed silently.

The truck rammed them from behind again, but instead of letting up, he continued to push them. Tack pressed the gas pedal, his jaw clenched and his eyes laser focused on the empty road ahead. A curve was coming, and his lips hardened into a straight line.

Chelsey glanced back, hoping for the ability to make out the driver, but the windows, including the windshield, were illegally tinted and she couldn't see. As Tack took the turn, the truck let up.

Chelsey's lungs felt like bricks. Fear coursed through her veins, as she knew full well that this was no scare tactic.

The truck began to pass but then rammed Tack's side with intensity, shoving their vehicle against the guardrail, sparks skidding as metal rode on metal.

"Hold on, hon," Tack said through a grunt as he maneuvered the vehicle to keep them from going over the edge.

One more ram of the monster truck did the job, and Chelsey shrieked. It happened so fast she couldn't keep up with the motions. Their truck flipped over the guardrail and plummeted.

A sharp stab filled her body, and she lost her breath. Tack's hand grabbed hers and squeezed as the truck rolled, the sound of crunching metal piercing her ears as it flipped then landed with a crash.

After that she saw nothing.

Chelsey's eyes popped open. The truck had landed upright, but the windows were shattered and the windshield was missing. Her head throbbed, and her body ached and roared in torment. She had small cuts and scrapes, but she could move—not without wincing, but nothing major appeared to be broken; her left wrist screamed in agony. Probably a fracture.

Tack was unconscious, limp over the steering wheel. Chelsey carefully touched his neck and felt for a pulse. He had one. "Tack," she said through a thick voice. He didn't move. Didn't wake. Where was her phone? She rummaged around using her right hand, that wrist throbbing, too. The phone must have fallen out of her purse, which was also missing. Tack's phone that he'd left in the holder under the radio had gotten lost in the wreck.

She huffed and grabbed her head. She was dazed and a little dizzy, but she had to fight through the fog. Sleepiness overtook her. So. Tired. She slumped in her seat as the passenger door opened.

"Help us. Help us, please," she mumbled as strong arms cradled her.

"Shh... I got ya."

She nodded. "Help him...he needs—"

"He'll be fine. You need to worry about you right now."

"Okay," she slurred. "But come back for Tackitt." She

tried to fight off the fatigue, but it did no good and she passed out in strong arms.

When she awoke, her arm hurt worse than before, and she tried to rub it, but it was bound behind her back. Panic jolted her awake, and her vision cleared.

She was in a small cabin. Sparse. Musty. She'd been tied to a ladder-back wooden chair. Her wrist screamed in protest. Willing the fog to clear, she began inventorying the room and calculating a plan to escape. The dirty windowpanes revealed desert terrain and mountains. Could be anywhere. Chelsey had no way to determine how long she'd been out or how far her captor had taken her.

Captor! She'd thought she'd been rescued.

The back door of the cabin swung open with a creak, and heavy footfalls thudded against the hardwood.

"Ah, you're awake."

And looking right into the eyes of Dusty Reddington. How had she missed the signs? Cocky. Thrill seeking. A risk taker who had access to ranches through his father's business as well as the rodeo circuit. He might have said he didn't know Maria, but knowing too many victims would have tipped off Chelsey, and he was smart enough to realize it.

He loved dominating and controlling an unruly bull.

"What did you do with Tack? He's your friend. You tried to kill him."

"I did not try to kill him. I was hoping for you. Figured you'd run slower than him, and he has expertise in the rodeo ring. Though, if it has to come to that, so be it." He tossed his cowboy hat on the counter, then knelt in front of her, his eyes dark and void of humanity. He'd been putting on the biggest facade, conning them all. Chelsey hadn't seen through it. Hadn't read her mark.

If she hadn't been second-guessing herself thanks to the taunts of a mass shooter who'd been all up in her head, as if he knew just what to say to deflate any confidence and self-esteem she had, she would have solidified the profile, and it would have pointed straight to Dusty.

"He could die out there."

"Maybe." He eyed her and cocked his head. "I thought the bulls would be my greatest opponent. Turns out it's a woman who weighs a buck ten with a smart mouth and a brain that actually works." He smacked the side of her head, not hard but not playfully, either. "Only a matter of time before you came sniffing me out. But I don't lose, remember?"

"Have you been behind all the attacks?"

He scowled. "You think that coward sending you letters has the ego, the courage to do anything else? He opened fire on helpless women working out. Where's the excitement in that? No one to feel the fear and know you're in control and have all the power. Senseless. That's what that was."

So the attacks with guns and otherwise were Dusty. Guess Jerry Allen had actually received a text. "You like the hunt. The excitement that you could get caught, but you never do. Because you're good at what you do. You weren't just talking about the rodeo the other day."

"No. Riding bulls keeps me satiated for a while, but then the thirst for a new hunt, a new thrill overtakes it." He grinned and grazed her cheek with his thumb. "I always thought you'd be good to take, but out of respect for Tack, I left you alone. When you came into the house that night Izzy was there, I thought the stars had aligned just for me."

"If you didn't know I was at the house, how did you know Izzy would be?"

He tapped his temple. "I'd been watching Izzy. Tracking her. I thought she'd been keeping the house clean and was stocking it for when I came back—which happened to be early, thanks to a tornado. I call that perfect timing."

"Except I came in."

"And that brought Tackitt. Which presented a problem and a fun challenge. Could I keep up appearances? Yes. Yes, I did."

"You don't think Tack will figure this out?" She worked her restraints, hoping to break free, but he was a cowboy and knew how to tie someone up right, unfortunately. If she could keep him talking, she might be able to figure a way out.

"Nah. He isn't sure who is after you exactly. I guess I do owe that weak-willed mass shooter a thank-you for keeping Tack—and you—confused. Tack was out cold when I took you. I'm not in the truck I normally drive. He's none the wiser."

Dusty was clever and rich enough to have more than one vehicle.

"You might be my greatest conquest and trophy."

Greatest trophy… Her wheels clicked. The women had been buried high on a mountain like a tall trophy—the highest honor. The circle of honor. That was the national trophy Dusty wanted, but these women he'd tortured and murdered were his greatest achievement. His true circle of honor, and that's why they were buried in a circle.

"The other victims?"

"Josephine, Maria, Carmella and Rosa. Then Izzy. Of course, I never had the chance to bring her to the circle. You ruined that. I had to kill her in the hospital." His put-out expression was like a stench in her nostrils. He was a narcissistic sociopath. No reasoning with one of those.

But she could appeal to his arrogance. "You going to have your way with me all bound up? You sneak up on helpless women, prey on those who can't fight. How is that any different than the mass shooter? That's not competitive or thrilling. Let me out of the stall. See if you can last eight seconds." This could backfire in a myriad of ways, and she was scared out of her mind, but she needed a cool, level head. Needed to be free of these restraints or there would be no fighting chance to survive.

He playfully clipped her chin with his knuckles, then leaned in and kissed her. "We got plenty of time," he whispered, and she spit on the floor. He laughed. "I like your fire and spirit." He stood and stretched as if it was a lazy afternoon with nothing pressing to do.

"Tack is going to find me."

"Doubtful. He doesn't even know about this old cabin. Why would he? It's secluded and private. Where I had planned to bring Izzy. Where I brought them all before burying them. I guess I'll find a new burial site. You'll be the first. But not the last." He stood. "I got some supplies I need to grab. Hang tight." He winked and left the cabin.

Chelsey worked the ropes on her arms and feet, the burn cutting into her flesh, and her wrist, which she was positive was now fully broken, sent a piercing stab so intense it rattled her brain; sweat broke out on her brow. She struggled and fought, but unless he freed her, she was going nowhere.

And if he strangled her first…

She and Tack hadn't made anything right. Chelsey was going to die, and Tack hadn't forgiven her. He wasn't a man to take that with a grain of salt, and he'd feel guilty forever.

Pride goes before a fall.

That truth returned to her heart. She'd been so focused on helping others to make up for Dad's sins that she'd allowed what she did to become who she was, and then her whole world and identity had rested in that. Tack had been right.

She profiled herself. An insecure woman who needed to feel secure and powerful because she'd been powerless as a child. A woman obsessed until it swallowed her whole, creating a need for perfectionism on her job—because her job was her. With every win and resulting accolade, she'd become puffed up—invincible. Like Dusty. And if she went even deeper, Chelsey had been competing with her own father's spotless con record.

She was a hot mess. "God, forgive me," she whispered. Instead of relying on God, she'd relied on herself. And it had royally backfired and bound her, just like these ropes.

Pride had led her to this fall, and if God didn't help her up, she'd end up six feet in the ground, like the other victims.

FOURTEEN

Tack ignored his excruciating condition. Chelsey was gone, and he wasn't sure who had her. The mass shooter? The Outlaw? When he'd come to, he'd found his cell phone, which had fallen out of the window upon impact, he guessed, and he called 911. There was a manhunt for Chelsey now. He'd called in his company for extra Ranger help and forgone the hospital, though he was certain he needed a couple of stitches on his chin, but every minute spent not looking for Chelsey was a minute he could lose her.

The very reason he pushed his feelings aside. Losing her would be more than he could handle, and yet here he was. Without her. His last words were ones that had severed their relationship. If he could take them all back, he would. She was on his mind always. Every good moment revolved around her… He stopped short as reality unraveled in his heart. No wonder Arlie broke things off and said it wasn't going to go anywhere between them. Everything there was to know about him involved Chelsey, and she'd seen it clearly. It was going nowhere because his entire life was wrapped up in another woman.

He'd talked to Jerry Allen, who was now in custody. He'd admitted to taking payment to help bring illegal immigrants into the country, but he'd never murdered anyone, and he didn't know who might be killing women. Tack wanted to believe him, but it was hard to know who was telling the truth and withholding it. Like Chelsey. He hadn't even accepted her apology, which he knew was sincere. He'd seen the guilt. And she'd tried to tell him once before.

Her words to him, to soothe and comfort him, returned to his heart when she'd placed a light kiss near his ear, the action moving and shifting places he'd kept locked up.

"Sometimes people do things we can't stop even if we want to stop them."

That was her way of revealing truth about herself, too. She hadn't been able to stop her dad, but she had wanted to.

Now, he walked into the ranch. Chelsey was a doodler and up most nights. She hadn't given him an official profile, but that didn't mean she wasn't working one secretly. It was a last-ditch effort as he waited for FBI agents to step in and help with the search. He'd called Chelsey's section chief, and he'd coordinated with all Texas field offices for help and was sending in two behavioral analysts who had knowledge of the case. They'd be arriving in less than an hour now. The sheriff's deputies were going back to the Sagets' as well as other places like the ranch management property to interview persons of interest. If one of them was missing, then that might be the tell.

He gathered up all her information and hurried back to the station, where he laid out all Chelsey's notes on a table in a conference room. "God, let there be something. Help me find her."

He organized the piles. Some notes were about the mass shooter, some about victims and others pertained to the Outlaw. Chelsey had written, scratched out and written again.

Thrill-seeker. Control. Narcissist. Possible God complex.

Hossy-stink. Rancher. Cowboy. She wrote Anthony Gonzalez and Brick Saget's names and then had written under each of them descriptions. Her list for Brick Saget was longer. They'd put out a BOLO on Anthony Gonzalez and picked him up twenty minutes ago. He denied being the Outlaw, attending the rodeo and abducting Chelsey. It was possible in all the panic of Tack getting tossed by a bull, Chelsey had seen someone and attached Anthony's physique and appearance to them. Because they likely were not Gonzalez.

The door opened, and a man loomed in the door frame. He was about the same height as Tack but beefier. His temples were silver, but his dark eyes were sharp. Tack guessed he was early to midforties. Tack stood.

"Special Agent Duke Jericho." A woman slipped in beside him. Petite, late thirties if he had to guess, dressed überconservative. He noticed red puckers on her right hand and wrist, but she was covered in long sleeves—wrong attire for this heat—and a few more puckers crept above her collar onto the right side of her neck, but her hair was down covering most of them. "This is Special Agent Vera Gilmore. We're here to assist with Chelsey's abduction."

While both stood stoic, there was concern for their colleague in their eyes.

"Please come in," Tack said and welcomed them with his hand. "I'm going over Chelsey's notes now."

"I feel like I need to be chomping ice to look at them," Agent Gilmore murmured, and Agent Jericho smirked.

"Fill us in," Agent Jericho said, and Tack told them everything he knew and where the investigation was leading.

"We're aware of the mass shooter. We've been re-working that profile, hoping for a new lead to pop." Agent Jericho inspected the notes. "These are a little vaguer than I'm used to seeing from her."

"Her ego took a hit," Agent Gilmore said. "She'd be timid in this one. Being too cautious for fear of making a mistake. But her instincts are excellent, so there will be something. Even a word. A sentence. Something notable. Insecurity doesn't erase natural ability. Hampers it. But it'll be there. Keep looking, Duke."

The agents peppered him with questions, some more personal than he would have liked, but they were doing the victimology. On his Chelsey.

Keep it together, Tackitt.

Agent Gilmore frowned. "What is hossy-stink?"

Agent Jericho patted her shoulder and explained, "He could be a cowboy. Rancher."

Vera cocked her head and picked up another stack of papers. "Bull rider?"

Tack's world tilted as he took the paper. Chelsey had written it, scratched it out, then written it again underneath with a question mark, then scratched it out, then circled it. It was her strongest feeling about the killer, but all her second-guessing had her questioning if she were right or not. She would have pinpointed Dusty had she not been confused and insecure.

The night Dusty gave them a ride, his truck had smelled of hossy-stink, and it must have triggered Chelsey's idea that the Outlaw was a bull rider. Dusty was well-known to everyone. Worked the local rodeos. Knew many of the ranchers nearby. Traveled.

"I may know who it is." He told them everything. Dusty fit the profile. His friend. Right under his nose. Tack had brought Chelsey here. To a killer's home. "But there's nothing in the ranch that would give indication. We combed it when Izzy and Chelsey were attacked."

He picked up the phone and called the Reddingtons. Maybe they could help with where Dusty might go for privacy when he wasn't on the ranch. A place he could hide a monster truck, his flashy everyday truck, plus the beat-up truck he'd been in that night he attacked Izzy and Chelsey.

After talking to Mr. Reddington, he ended the call. "I know where she might be."

Chelsey only had one choice. A punishing one. Her ankles were tied to the legs of the chair. But she could stand, hunched over. That meant she might get some power or momentum. If she could hurl the chair to the floor, she might be able to break it and free herself from it. It was heavy enough and rickety already. That's when she spotted Dusty's wallet and keys and pocketknife on the coffee table.

Time wasn't on her side. Adrenaline kicked in as she worked to scoot the chair across the floor. A little bit at a time, she inched her way over until she was at the coffee table. But it was too short for her to grab the keys.

She had one shot. A long shot.

Moving closest to the knife, she tipped the chair backward, falling into the table and grabbing the knife in her fall. Her head banged against the wooden chair and the thud jerked her arms, sending a new stabbing sensation into her wrist, but she had the knife.

Lying on her side, she worked the knife open and began cutting the ropes. She sawed with intensity and felt the give. Free! She hurried and cut the ropes on her feet, grabbed his truck keys then sprinted out the back door.

She kept low and listened, unsure of where Dusty had gone. She tiptoed around the cabin toward the truck parked out front and heard voices. Two men. One was Dusty. "If you think I'm going to let you kill her, you're crazy," the voice she didn't fully recognize said, but there was familiarity.

A scuffle sounded, then gunfire startled her. She crept around to peek and saw Dusty on the ground and the back of a man standing over him. She was rescued.

Standing, she moved forward, and brush underneath her crunched. The man swung around and spotted her, then smiled. "And here I thought you might need some help getting free from this loon."

Something didn't feel right. Why was Donna Saget's son Eddie Rodriguez standing before her? "What's going on?" she asked warily.

"I saw this guy push you off the road, after you left the house. I left, too. Followed him back here and was planning on being the cavalry."

Hairs spiked on her neck. She knew this voice. Knew the face. Not because he was her celebrity crush's look-alike. Where? "Why didn't you call the police?"

"I like being the hero?" He shrugged and aimed the gun on her. "And I thought I'd introduce myself properly to you. You might know me as Ward Rodriguez. Only my mom and her little minions call me Eddie."

Ward. Rodriguez. She'd once reviewed his recorded interview. "Your stepsister managed Warrior Women Gym. In Dallas." Unbelievable. "You told the PD that there was footage of Marty Stockton stalking women outside the Warrior Women Gym—women who had been harassed by him at previous gyms." That's why they'd found an all-women's place. So he couldn't come in. But he'd lingered outside. Marty had fit the profile.

"I see your confusion. My sister found out I was embezzling money and was going to the owner. She said if I was on the take there, then her daddy needed to know, because I was probably stealing from him, too. I had to stop her."

"You murdered a host of women to simply cover up a vendetta against one woman. Why would you have sent me letters to taunt me? You could have gotten away with it."

He grinned. "Yeah. I could have. But see, that's not the only reason. Marty was messing around on my turf. He had no idea how to hunt a woman, get inside her head, make her think she was going crazy. He had no idea how to incite fear. But I do. I been doing it a long time."

Eddie had been psychologically torturing the pool of women at the gym. He'd gotten rid of his sister in a way that wouldn't point back to him and accused Marty in one fell swoop. He could still embezzle and terrorize women.

"I did it to you. Your facial reaction on camera when they came to the hospital was priceless. I knew you were ready—at the bottom. Done."

Taunting her wasn't the game. It was the beginning of what he had planned. She was no safer with Eddie than she was with Dusty. He motioned her back into the cabin.

"How did you find me in Virginia and here?"

"It isn't hard to discover if you have any skills. You should know this. Imagine my surprise when I found out your ticket was to El Paso. Yes, I have hacking ability." He bowed as if she should be so impressed. "I followed you and the Texas Ranger. You were right here beside me! Perfection. Then this idiot thought he could horn in on all my work? Like Marty. I don't think so." His eyes darkened. "Inside. Now."

She didn't move. If he got close enough, she could disable him, take the gun. She'd been trained. He didn't seem to mind the fact she was disobeying. He closed the distance between them.

The sound of vehicles turned their attention. She went for the gun, he dodged and grabbed her in a choke hold, putting the gun to her head. Pulse pounding, she went silent as an SUV bounded up and her friends Duke Jericho and Vera Gilmore jumped out. Tack rounded the hood with his gun aimed at Eddie Rodriguez.

"I'll kill her!"

"I've kind of heard this before," Tack said, and she actually smiled for fear she might break down and lose it all right here and now. She'd been attacked for days. Mentally strained. Afraid. Anxious. "Let's talk about it."

Duke kept his weapon trained on Eddie, too. "Now, you do see you're outnumbered. You seem like a smart man who can count. At least to three."

Great. Two smart alecks.

Vera huffed. "Let her go and we can talk our way out of the death penalty."

Tack inched forward. Eddie pressed the gun farther into her head.

"Hey, Chels, remember that snake?"

What snake? Eddie's hand trembled. He was going to do it. He was going to shoot her and they'd shoot him, but she'd be dead. "No." Was this a stalling tactic? There wasn't time. Eddie had weighed his options. She heard the resigned sigh.

"Yeah, you do, hon. Right after the horse threw you." He never let his eyes leave Eddie's face.

Right after the horse...yes. "You—" He'd shot it. A hair from her hand. Oh, but this wasn't her hand. It was her head!

"You can shoot me if you want," Eddie said. "But not before I shoot—"

Gunfire.

Heat whizzed by her face, and Eddie dropped to the ground dead, a bullet to the head.

FIFTEEN

Chelsey had packed her bags an hour ago. Last night after Tack shot and killed Eddie Rodriguez, she had been taken to the hospital and treated for a broken wrist. Tack took three stitches to his chin. But they were alive. Afterward, they'd gone back to the ranch, where Duke and Vera encouraged her to return to Quantico. She was needed, missed and no one had lost any respect for her. She'd needed to hear that. To hear truth after so many lies.

Out there listening to Dusty, she'd realized she was more like him than she wanted to be. After Duke and Vera left, she'd called her dad. She loved him, crazy as it might sound, but he was toxic. He'd never hurt her. Never failed to provide or even buoy her self-esteem. Never once said a negative thing about her. But he'd exploited her. And she was done with him. He hadn't taken it well. Especially when she told him she'd told Tack what he'd done.

He knew Tack would look into it. Send it up to White-Collar Crimes. He wasn't that good. There would be a paper trail. Her misguided love and guilt had kept her silent. No more. If she had to leave the Bureau, so be it.

She'd hung up and fallen asleep and hadn't seen Tack this morning. Yet. He'd taken the shot. Made the shot. Saved her again. Looking at the Bible she always brought with her but never read, she opened it.

I count not myself to have apprehended it, but this one thing I do: forgetting those things which are behind, and reaching forth unto those things which are before... Philippians 3:13 leaped off the page and into her heart.

She couldn't wallow in the past. She'd never forget it, but staying there did no one any good. It was time to reach for the future. What would that look like?

Did she even want to go back to Quantico? She did love building profiles. While her father had helped her hone those skills to take advantage of people, God had used them for good. But as much as she hated being shot at, she enjoyed fieldwork. If she transferred, she would have to go to Washington or Maryland first until space at a field office in Texas opened up. That could take a while.

A light knock brought her from her thoughts, and her pulse spiked as Tack stepped inside the room, noticing the Bible on her lap. He grinned. "You finding the right verses to make your case in forgiving me?"

She laid the Bible on the bed and stood. "Me forgive you? For what? Grazing my cheek with a bullet?" she teased. Why would she need to forgive him? He'd done nothing wrong.

"For my hurtful words. For writing off your friendship when I was furious. Also, I once put a dead mouse in your locker."

"That was—never mind." She'd get paybacks later. "You had every right—"

"I had no rights." He crossed to her in three strides. "You've been my best friend for as long as I can remember. You are not responsible for your dad's actions. Justice will be served to him."

"You're not mad at me anymore?"

"No."

She grinned, feeling lighter inside. Time to tell the truth. No more secrets. "Good. Because I love you."

His mouth turned south at those words. "I know."

She touched his cheek. "No, you don't. Let me rephrase. I am *in* love with you, Tackitt Holliday. I've always been in love with you. I compare every single man to you, which is why nothing has ever worked out. There's nobody for me but you, and I got scared. I knew you'd be angry and turn me away, so I never told you until it ate at me too much not to. I—I don't deserve you."

His eyes filled with moisture, and he turned away, as if her seeing his emotion would weaken him. For a man like Tack, tears would be an enemy. "Tack, look at me."

He faced her. "I'm not the rock you think I am."

"I don't think you're a rock. I think you're a strong and brave man who feels deeply, but you cover it up with tough guy stuff."

"Did you just profile me?"

"I believe I did." She smiled.

"I'm in love with you, too," he murmured. "Kissing you never felt like kissing a sister."

"Good to hear." She beamed. "And I never thought kissing you felt like kissing a brother."

"I've been afraid of loving for fear of losing. But when you were kidnapped, all I could think about was time I wasted. Time I want with you. I don't want Charlotte—though she may just want me for my bone structure—or anybody else, for that matter. I just want you. And we'll make it work somehow. I'll come to Virginia."

"I was thinking of coming back to Texas."

"Can't get the Texas out of you?" He framed her face.

"And the man I love lives here. I thought maybe I'd settle down, as much as one like me can, buy a little ranch. Grow old. Ride some horses—"

His lips meeting hers cut her off, and he kissed her like a man who knew just what he wanted—forever. "You had me at 'I'm in love with you.'" He kissed her again, this time with more intensity, greater longing. She could live here in this kiss. In this moment. "But I do love the ranch idea. Growing old together."

"Maybe making a couple of babies," she offered.

"Long as they get your brains and beauty. And my sense of humor." He kissed her again. "Chelsey Holliday. I like it." He pulled back and peered deep into her eyes. "I'm going to propose, honey. But I want to do it when I have a ring and it doesn't kill me to dip onto my knee."

She laughed. They were physically a mess right now. "Well, spoiler alert. I'm going to say yes."

He pulled her tight against him. "Good. I'd hate to have to shoot ya for saying no. I am a crack shot, you know."

"You're going to rub that in for the rest of our lives, aren't you?" she asked as they walked down the hall, his arm swinging around her shoulder as she leaned into him.

"If it wasn't for me," he said, "we wouldn't have the rest of our lives."

"That answers that question." Before she could continue to protest, he swept her into a kiss that made her forget what she was going to say anyway. It didn't matter.

She was with the man she'd loved her whole life, teasing and all. She'd take it and never let go.

* * * * *

Watch for more books in
Jessica R. Patch's Quantico Profilers miniseries,
coming soon from Love Inspired Suspense.

And be sure to pick up
Her Darkest Secret *by Jessica R. Patch,*
new from Love Inspired Trade,
available April 2022 exclusively at Walmart!

Dear Reader,

First, thank you for being gracious if you're familiar with Mariscal Canyon. I did take some geographical liberty to fit the story, and of course Gran Valle is fictional. And thank you for reading Chelsey and Tack's story. Chelsey struggled with relying on herself and her skill and ability to be the very best to the point of perfectionism. But we are not a perfect people and make mistakes. Due to her overachieving nature and pride, she took a mistake and made it into a career killer. Maybe you struggle with the need to be perfect and are too hard on yourself when you make a mistake. Give yourself some grace, stay humble and rely on God—the source of our strength and all wisdom.

I'd love to connect with you! Join me at BookBub, https://www.bookbub.com/authors/jessica-r-patch, and sign up for my "Patched In" newsletter to receive exclusive book news and a "Patch of Hope" monthly devotion at www.jessicarpatch.com.

Jessica

COMING NEXT MONTH FROM
Love Inspired Suspense

DETECTION DETAIL
Rocky Mountain K-9 Unit • by Terri Reed
Protecting an alleged arsonist was not what K-9 officer Nelson Rivers
and accelerant-detection dog, Diesel, expected from any assignment.
But when a gunman targets Mia Turner, Nelson will need to figure out if
she's guilty or innocent—before she's hunted down.

HIGH-RISK RESCUE
Honor Protection Specialists • by Elizabeth Goddard
Surviving a shoot-out is not how Hannah Kahn planned to start her new
job. But when her boss is killed, she'll have to rely on Ayden Honor—her
boss's bodyguard and her ex—to outrun the mysterious mercenaries
now intent on chasing her...

ABDUCTION IN THE DARK
Range River Bounty Hunters • by Jenna Night
When kidnappers force their way into her house to abduct her nephew,
Tanya Rivera will do anything to protect him, even if it makes her
their new target. Teaming up with bounty hunter Danny Ryan, who is
tracking one of the men, might be her only chance at evading their
clutches and keeping everyone safe...

WITNESS IN PERIL
by Jodie Bailey
Narrowly escaping an attack by a man wearing a US Marshals badge,
estate lawyer Ivy Bridges flees to the one man she can trust—her ex,
Special Agent Jacob Garcia. And discovering her child is *his* daughter
makes him even more determined to stop the killer on her heels.

MOUNTAIN MURDER INVESTIGATION
Smoky Mountain Defenders • by Karen Kirst
While attempting to expose a cheating ring at the university that has
left one student dead, architecture professor Aiden Ferrer turns to
ex-fiancée mounted officer Raven Hart for help—except she thinks he's
dead. Will they be able to outrun a murderer *and* their feelings?

CANYON SURVIVAL
by Connie Queen
When Annie Tillman wakes on a cliff with amnesia, two small children
at her side and someone shooting at her, she knows she must run.
Former FBI agent Riggs Brenner rescues them and now he's her best
hope of surviving in the canyon—and recovering her memories.

LOOK FOR THESE AND OTHER LOVE INSPIRED BOOKS WHEREVER
BOOKS ARE SOLD, INCLUDING MOST BOOKSTORES, SUPERMARKETS,
DISCOUNT STORES AND DRUGSTORES.

LISCNM0222

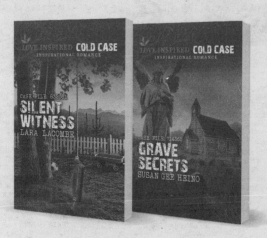